Sam was so beautiful. So masculine. The glow of the mask giving him an otherworldly appearance that only added to his appeal.

Ruby's breathing altered, becoming choppy as they stared at each other. She tried to shake her head to clear her senses, but his fingers prevented her from breaking eye contact with him. Irrationally, she felt light-headed, drunk on the clean, intoxicating scent of musk and man. Then his other hand sought the nape of her neck and she didn't know if he leaned down farther or she stretched upward, but suddenly his lips were on hers, warm and firm and utterly compelling.

Wide-eyed, she met his stunned gaze and then she couldn't help herself; she lowered her eyelids and opened her mouth. She heard a deep groan rumble out of his chest as he felt her submit to the inevitable and he slanted his lips more fully across hers to deepen the kiss. It burned through her like liquid fire, drugging her, consuming her, triggering an avalanche of need deep inside she was powerless to resist.

With two university degrees and a variety of false career starts under her belt, **Michelle Conder** decided to satisfy her lifelong desire to write and finally found her dream job. She currently lives in Melbourne, Australia, with one super-indulgent husband, three self-indulgent (but exquisite) children, a menagerie of overindulged pets and the intention of doing some form of exercise daily. She loves to hear from her readers at michelleconder.com.

Books by Michelle Conder

Harlequin Presents

Duty at What Cost?
The Most Expensive Lie of All
Hidden in the Sheikh's Harem
Defying the Billionaire's Command
The Italian's Virgin Acquisition

Conveniently Wed!

Bound to Her Desert Captor

The Chatsfield

Socialite's Gamble
Russian's Ruthless Demand

One Night With Consequences

Girl Behind the Scandalous Reputation
Prince Nadir's Secret Heir

Visit the Author Profile page
at Harlequin.com for more titles.

Michelle Conder

THE BILLIONAIRE'S VIRGIN TEMPTATION

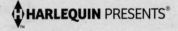

HARLEQUIN PRESENTS®

Recycling programs
for this product may
not exist in your area.

ISBN-13: 978-1-335-47824-5

The Billionaire's Virgin Temptation

First North American publication 2019

Copyright © 2019 by Michelle Conder

Printed in U.S.A.

www.Harlequin.com

THE BILLIONAIRE'S VIRGIN TEMPTATION

To Hilary and Marnie, writing partners in crime.

Thanks for the late nights out talking shop, eating divine food and drinking great wine.

Chin Chin is calling again!

Love always, M.C.

PROLOGUE

SAM FELT UNACCOUNTABLY agitated as he boarded his jet bound for Sydney. It was later than he would have liked and he was impatient to get underway.

'Will you be requiring dinner service during the flight, Mr Ventura?'

Sam folded his powerful frame into one of the leather tub chairs and tossed his mobile phone onto the table beside him before addressing his co-pilot. 'No, thanks, Daniel. Just a Scotch.'

'Certainly, sir.'

The flight from LA to Sydney would take about fourteen hours, give or take, during which Sam planned to catch up on work and sleep before he had to hit the ground running the following day. Not an uncommon occurrence for him.

Delivering his Scotch, the co-pilot headed back to the cockpit to prepare for take-off, leaving Sam to nurse his crystal tumbler and uncharacteristic edginess. As a general rule he wasn't the kind of person to second-guess himself once a decision had been made, but the question had crossed his mind more than once as to whether relocating to Sydney was the best thing to do right now.

He had a good life in LA. He surfed regularly, had a thriving legal practice that spanned two continents, lived on a great property on Malibu Beach and had any number of beautiful women he could call upon when he was in the mood for company—all drawn to the combination of power, money and good looks he'd been told he had in abundance.

Not that any of that mattered to his family, who were over the moon that he was returning home. After two years living in the City of Angels they were of the belief that he should settle back in his hometown and were more than happy with his decision to merge his highly successful legal practice with a large Australian enterprise.

The idea had been presented to him by his old university pal, Drew Kent, during a late-night dinner. Drew's father was retiring and Drew didn't want to take on the running of their law firm by himself. He was all about work-life balance ever since he'd married, and Sam, who had been in the market for a new challenge, had readily agreed to the idea.

He stared out at the night-dark sky as the plane banked hard to the right. Marriage had a way of changing a man's perspective on life. He'd seen it happen with colleagues at work and even his own brother, who had fallen in love and then, twelve months ago, got married. Valentino had gone from confirmed bachelor to happily married man with a baby faster than Sam's Maserati could hit a hundred clicks. Since then Tino had been unfailingly devoted to his lovely wife and son.

Was that what had set off the restlessness inside of him? The fact that Valentino was married and happy about it? Not that Sam begrudged Tino his happiness; quite the contrary. He loved seeing his older brother so fulfilled, and maybe one day he'd even take the plunge into matrimony himself. One day in the distant future when he met a woman who wasn't either completely obsessed with her own career, or the potential lifestyle his could provide for her.

Of its own accord his mind travelled back to the night, two years ago, when Valentino had met Miller, his now wife. Sam and Tino had been catching up in a Sydney bar when a stunning blonde in come-take-me stilettos had approached them. Ruby Clarkson had introduced herself and explained how Miller needed a date for an up-and-coming business event. Tino had jumped at the chance to help her best friend, leaving Sam and the blonde woman at a loose end. Since they both worked for the same law firm, but had never met, they'd spent the night talking shop and trading war stories until the bar had closed and kicked them out. Not wanting the night to end, Sam had offered to walk Ruby home and that was when the trouble had started.

His blood heated predictably at the memory of what had happened outside her apartment building. Or what had *nearly* happened outside her apartment building. Despite being incredibly attracted to her, he'd meant only to bid her goodnight, tell her it had been nice to meet her and good luck with her current case, but somehow she'd ended up in his arms and as soon as his lips had touched hers he'd been lost. She'd lit a flame in him that had only been doused when a neighbour had come out on to her balcony calling for her errant cat.

Later his brother would tell him that he had looked as if he'd been hit over the head with a golf club when he'd first caught sight of Ruby at the bar, and Tino had been right. From the moment Sam's dark eyes had collided with her wide-spaced intelligent green ones he'd completely lost his train of thought.

It had been the same at Miller and Tino's wedding just last year. He'd taken one look at Ruby in her dusky pink bridesmaid gown with the tantalising thigh-high split and decided to hell with it, he'd finish what they'd started the night they'd met and be done with it. That was until her date, some urbane banker-type, had stepped up beside her and ruined that particular fantasy.

Sam had downed a glass of champagne he hadn't wanted and told himself to forget it. Told himself that it was for the best. Ruby was his new sister-in-law's best friend and nothing good would come of them having a brief affair and things becoming potentially awkward later on down the track. Instead he'd forced himself to become interested in a gorgeous Sydney socialite and he'd been about to leave with her when Ruby had come rushing back into the reception room.

A small smile played at the edges of his lips. She'd been in such a flap she hadn't seen him at first and Sam hadn't stepped out of her path, choosing instead to let her run headlong into the circle of his arms as if he were just as startled by the contact as she was.

She'd stared up at him, a beguiling combination of sophistication and innocence, her gorgeous body pressed against his like Velcro on felt, her breathing laboured, and the memory of the night he'd nearly devoured her shining brightly in her lovely green eyes. For a split second his overly active imagination had caused him to believe that she'd come rushing back to find him. To tell him that she'd ditched her date and wanted to leave with him. Wanted to take him back to her place for the 'coffee' he'd stupidly passed up on the night they'd first met.

Then his oldest brother, Dante, had walked into the empty room and completely obliterated the moment.

'Sam, we're leav— Uh…sorry, junior, am I interrupting something?' he'd said smoothly.

Considering Sam had been a breath away from finding out if Ruby still tasted as delicious as he remembered, of course his brother had been interrupting, and the big idiot had known it!

Ruby's eyes had gone from glazed to mortified in the space of a heartbeat and she'd pushed out of his arms just as her date had arrived to find out what had delayed her.

Extreme sexual attraction, Sam had wanted to tell the other man.

Ruby had mumbled something about her jacket, quickly grabbed it from the back of her chair and hadn't looked back as she'd walked away. She'd been cool to him the whole day, he remembered now, and he often wondered why that was.

He also wondered what it was about her that made his libido override his iron-clad self-control where she was concerned, but he knew he'd work it out one day. And, given their shared profession, and personal connections, it would probably be soon.

His heart pounded slow and heavy inside his chest just at the thought of seeing her again. He'd deliberately not asked Valentino about her over the past couple of years. Why give his loved-up brother any indication that he had a thing for the beautiful lawyer? He'd only make more out of it than there was and the last thing Sam wanted was to raise Miller's awareness of how attractive he found her best friend.

But their paths would surely cross and he was curious as to how he would feel about her when it happened. Who knew, perhaps the incendiary attraction that sent his system into overdrive whenever she was in the room would have finally worn off? He'd lost interest in plenty of other women before. Surely Ruby wouldn't be any different in the end.

He swirled the Scotch in his glass. Did Ruby still

remember the night they'd met? Did she still think about it? And did she still work for Clayton Smythe or had she moved on to new pastures? He'd left the firm himself shortly after that night to start his own practice in LA and had ruthlessly suppressed all interest in her, so he had no idea what she was up to now. Some sixth sense warned him that, for all her bold confidence, Ruby was a soft touch deep down and therefore not to be trifled with. Not that he planned to trifle with her on any level. It would be pointless in the end and Sam had stopped chasing pointless passions after watching his world-famous father chase his motor-racing dreams to the exclusion of all else.

Theirs had never been a close relationship, his father dying in a tragic racing accident before Sam had been able to gain his attention or his approval—though God knew he'd wasted enough time trying to win both. He still remembered the time he'd trailed his father around the racetrack on his ninth birthday. It had been a disaster waiting to happen. He'd sat there all day, waiting to spend time with his father, only to have his old man drive off at the end of the day without him. As usual his father had been so preoccupied with work he'd completely forgotten Sam was even there. Fortunately one of the office girls had eventually noticed him sitting on a sofa, swinging his legs, and called his father on the phone. Sam had then been stuck in a taxi and delivered home alone.

His mother had been furious with his father but

Sam had brushed it off. That had been the last time his father had kicked his pride to the kerb, Sam had made sure of it. Not that it mattered now. He'd learned a valuable lesson that day and he'd never hung himself out to dry like that again. Never made anything so important that he couldn't walk away from it at the end of the day.

'A good thing,' he muttered into the ensuing silence, pulling out his phone and switching his mind from the past, where it didn't belong, to the present, where it did.

He was due to arrive in Sydney around noon and head straight into meetings with his new business partner before changing into some fancy-dress costume for a party he'd promised to attend.

A few months back he'd won a huge copyright case for Gregor Herzog and his wife—Australia's darling couple of the theatre world—when someone had tried to pass the couple's costume designs off as their own. Over the course of the case the Herzogs had become firm friends and they had invited him to their annual masquerade ball—a huge charity extravaganza that just happened to coincide with Gregor's fiftieth birthday celebration this year.

'Please come, Sam, my good friend. It would be an honour to raise a toast to you on my birthday.'

Sam already regretted his somewhat rash agreement to attend but a promise was a promise and Sam's word was his law.

Fortunately, he rarely suffered jet lag, but still,

he hoped that Gregor and Marion wouldn't mind if he only made a fly-in and fly-out appearance. What with family obligations to fulfil the rest of the weekend, and a new company to take control of on Monday morning, he didn't have a lot of time for frivolities like masquerade balls. Or thinking about gorgeous blondes with long legs, he mused, that strange, restless feeling returning as Ruby Clarkson once again jumped into his head.

He shook her image loose, unfolded his large frame from the chair and fetched his laptop from where his co-pilot had stowed it prior to take-off. The fact that the woman could turn him on from twelve thousand miles away should be mildly disconcerting—and it was! It made him realise that at some point he was going to have to figure out how to get the troublesome blonde out of his head. Something he hoped to put off for as long as possible.

CHAPTER ONE

THE THEME ON the gold-leaf invitation for Sydney's most renowned masquerade ball this year had been 'daring, romantic, seductive…'

Tick, tick and *tick*, Ruby thought, stifling a yawn and giving a smile she hoped conveyed *Having a great time* and not *I wish I was sipping this glass of Riesling at home on my sofa in front of the latest instalment of* Law & Order.

And wearing comfy pyjamas, Ruby mused longingly as she took in the packed ornate ballroom.

A lavish ball was the last place she wanted to be after a gruelling eighty-hour working week that had gone from bad to worse and still required more hours to be put in, but she was here in support of her sister, so leaving wasn't an option just yet.

And she supposed it was an interesting interlude from her everyday life sitting in her poky little law office, fighting the good fight. When else would she get the chance to join the who's who of the theatre world in a multimillion-dollar Point Piper mansion with unrivalled harbour views beyond the infinity pool?

Everywhere Ruby looked there was a dazzling display of elaborately costumed guests milling about and talking in a profusion of excitement and colour. It was like stepping back in time with women in wigs and masks and men with feather-plumed hats drinking impossibly elegant flutes of champagne that sparkled like liquid gold beneath the light of a thousand chandeliers. Frescoes of cherubs and deer stared down from the ceiling and the iconic gun-metal-grey Sydney Harbour Bridge glowed through the open French doors, reminding everyone that they were in fact in Sydney and not visiting some Venetian mansion on the banks of the Grand Canal during *Carnevale*.

Ruby surreptitiously adjusted the neckline of her fitted gown, which kept slipping to reveal a little too much cleavage for her liking. She was supposed to be Marie Antoinette but her mirror had deemed that she looked more like Little Bo Peep on steroids, making her thankful she was well-hidden behind an elaborate black lace mask.

'You know I really appreciate you coming along with me tonight, don't you?' Molly murmured.

Thanks to live music from the twenty-piece band where a well-known pop star was belting out her latest hit, Ruby had to lean in close to catch her sister's words.

'I'm enjoying myself,' she fibbed, not wanting

Molly to feel guilty about roping her into accompanying her. Molly was on a personal quest to waylay some in-demand director and convince him that she really needed to star in his next award-winning Hollywood epic. Molly had paid her dues at drama school and appeared in small-to-medium theatre productions and TV shows, and Ruby would do anything to help make her sister's dreams come true.

'No, you're not,' Molly said, shrugging good-naturedly. 'But I appreciate the lie. I'm also under strict instructions to make sure you have fun and relax for once.'

'Let me guess.' Ruby gave her sister *that* look, knowing full well where her instructions had come from. 'Mum told you to find me a nice man I can fall in love with so I can produce lots of grandbabies.' Nothing new there. 'Which is so not going to happen, and, for the record, I take serious umbrage at the insinuation that I don't normally relax and have fun because I do. All the time!'

'Oh, did I only insinuate that last bit?' Molly feigned a shocked expression. 'I meant to say it outright.'

'Ha-ha.' Ruby narrowed her eyes menacingly. 'I know how to relax.' She had a yoga class booked the following morning, didn't she? '*And* how to have fun.'

'You work,' Molly corrected. 'But that's okay. Tonight I will ply you with drinks and ensure that you meet some tall, dark and handsome man to while the evening away with.'

Ruby grimaced. As any self-respecting lawyer knew, weekend work was par for the course. Particularly with the big cases, and Ruby had just embarked on one of the biggest of her career, so men were not a priority for her right now. If they ever had been.

'You can't tell if a man is handsome or not while he's wearing a mask,' Ruby pointed out, 'and you already know that I don't hold to Mum's mantra that a woman isn't complete without a man on her arm.'

'Mum is old-school,' Molly agreed. 'You can't hold that against her.'

'I don't hold it against her. I'm just not intending to follow in her footsteps.'

'By not dating at all?'

'I date,' Ruby defended, tucking a recalcitrant strand of her blonde hair back under her poufy white wig. 'When I have the time.'

Molly gave her a good-natured eye-roll. 'The last time you went on a date, dinosaurs roamed the earth.'

Ruby laughed at the visual. 'I'm not a romantic like you and Mum. I don't see "the one" in every man who looks my way.'

'That's because you never give any guy a decent chance. You find something wrong with all of them and quickly move on. But seriously, Rubes, just because Dad left Mum for another woman it doesn't mean every man will do the same to us.'

Ruby couldn't deny that their father's desertion

had left her somewhat jaded when it came to romance, but that wasn't the only reason. In her experience men wanted more from a woman than they were prepared to give and she had yet to meet a man who challenged that theory.

Even Sam Ventura.

Especially Sam Ventura—even if he now was her best friend's brother-in-law.

And why did his name leap into her head every time the conversation turned to men and marriage? He was the very last man she should be thinking about in that way. Two years ago he'd charmed her and kissed her senseless before making a trite promise to call and then failing to follow through on it.

Not that she should have been surprised. She'd been taken in by his good looks and intelligent conversation, but neither of those things was a precursor to nice manners and true decency. At least not where he was concerned!

Lord, but it still made her blush to recall how she had invited him up to her apartment for coffee.

Coffee!

She might as well have just said *bed* and been done with it.

His failure to call and the subsequent photo she'd seen of him with his arm around another woman the following day at a polo match had solidified for her that men weren't worth the effort. The worst thing for Ruby was that she had let Sam *in* that night. She'd let down her guard with him in a way she never had before, and worse, she'd thought they'd shared a connection. A connection that had transcended the physical.

Fool that she was.

She'd found out via a visiting LA attorney that Sam had a reputation for being a charming rogue who made Casanova look like a good bet. Something she wholeheartedly believed after how easily he had nearly seduced her that night. He'd made her feel like a besotted thirteen-year-old in the throes of her first crush, carrying her phone around for a whole week, waiting for a phone call he'd never intended to make.

Her extreme reaction to him was something that had scared her witless because she had always imagined herself immune to the romantic vagaries that governed her mother's life. She supposed she had Sam to thank for showing her otherwise. Showing her that if she wasn't careful she could be just as susceptible to a pretty face and buff body as the next woman.

Not that she *would* thank him. She didn't want to have anything to do with him again. He was too big and too male and definitely too full of himself to be of interest to her. Something she hoped she'd made crystal clear by ignoring him at Tino and Miller's wedding last year.

'I don't think every man is an EC,' she denied to Molly now, using their shorthand for Emotional Coward. 'But I do wonder how we're even sisters.

You're like Snow White, talking to all the animals and skipping through the flowery fields, and I'm—'

'The Wicked Queen,' Molly filled in. 'Only you're not afraid of ageing, you're afraid of commitment.'

'I am not afraid of commitment.'

Molly's eyebrow rose above her white mask as if to say *I'm not getting into that argument again*. But it wasn't true.

'I'm cautious,' Ruby countered. 'I don't feel the need to leap into something before I've had a chance to study it from all angles.'

'You're not supposed to study love,' Molly laughed. 'You feel it. You experience it. You *live* it.'

Ruby shuddered. 'You might. I don't.' And what would Molly say, she wondered, if she knew Ruby hadn't even gone all the way with a man yet? That she was still a virgin like an old maid from the Victorian era!

Suddenly a loud honking sound drew her attention. Molly giggled as an irate swan cut a swathe through the glittering crowd and started pecking at the golden tassels hanging from an unsuspecting woman's gown. The woman reeled back and would have slipped if the man standing beside her hadn't put his hands out and swiftly caught her.

Ruby felt the breath back up in her lungs as she took in the man's height and the breadth of his shoulders, the angle of his leonine head and dark hair styled in loose layers that could only have come from an upmarket salon.

'Oh, my,' Molly murmured. 'Would you get a load of that?'

Ruby watched as the man wearing a masculine bronze mask competently corralled the indignant bird outside and returned to check if the woman was okay.

'He's gorgeous,' her sister added on a sigh.

'You can't possibly know that,' Ruby scoffed. 'He's wearing a mask that covers half his face.'

'He carries himself like a man who doesn't need to be handsome but is. Look at those shoulders—'

'Padding.'

'And the way his thighs fill out his dark suit trousers. No padding there, I'm guessing.'

Despite Ruby's protestations, Molly was right—the man exuded power and confidence and his square-cut jaw, smooth olive complexion and sensual mouth conveyed that he was likely very good-looking behind the bronzed mask. He was also very familiar…

It's not him, she assured herself, her eyes taking in the way his lips twisted into a half-cynical, half-sexy grin as the grateful woman gripped his arm and whispered something into his ear.

It couldn't be him. Sam Ventura lived in LA and, even if he was visiting Sydney, what would he be doing at a fancy-dress ball thrown by theatre people?

Well, he wouldn't be here, she reasoned. It was her imagination running overtime. Again. 'Men like that only want one thing from a woman,' she told Molly with lofty finality.

'I know.' Molly sighed. 'Do you think he would want it from me?'

'Molly!'

Ruby was saved from reminding her sister that she'd just ended a relationship with one feckless boyfriend and hardly needed another when one of Molly's friends approached her. Perturbed by how very much the dark-haired man reminded her of Sam Ventura, Ruby offered to go to the bar, where they were serving on-demand cocktails.

'Cosmopolitan,' Molly requested.

'Same,' her friend added.

Leaving them to their excited chatter, Ruby headed for the gilt-edged bar that looked as if it was a permanent fixture but was most likely shipped in from Italy especially for the night.

She sighed as she joined the queue at the bar. Molly truly believed that love awaited her around every corner, while Ruby was of the view that danger awaited her. She wasn't looking for romance and happy-ever-after. Her independence had been too hard-won to hand over to some man who would want her to compromise everything she had and then most likely walk away without a backward glance anyway. A man like her father. And like Sam Ventura.

No, that wasn't fair. She might not like Sam very much but she didn't know him well enough to tar him with her father's particular brush. Still, why give a man who had *heartbreaker* written all over his too handsome face the chance to prove that he was? And why was he still on her mind? she wondered grouchily.

Love turned thinking women into veritable psych-ward patients, she knew that. Just look at how she had been after only kissing the man that one fool-hardy night. He'd pulled her into his arms and she'd nearly lost her dignity and her panties in one fell swoop! Not that she'd been in love with him, but she'd certainly been in lust with him and that had been more than enough to keep her up late some nights.

'Sorry, darling,' a male voice crooned too close to her ear as she was jostled from behind. Ruby glanced over her shoulder and caught a glimpse of four co-lourful characters wearing Zorro-style masks with their eyes on her cleavage.

Very original, she thought, turning away and stead-fastly ignoring them as she waited for the woman in front of her to collect her drinks order. If there was one valuable lesson Ruby had learned from watching her mother all these years, it was not to let her emo-tions do the thinking for her. Only fools rushed in and when they did they were often sorry with the results.

'So I said, listen, doll-face.' The guy who had jostled her spoke behind her with an over-the-top drawl. 'You want it, you know where to find it. On your knees.'

His companions guffawed as if they were smug

private school boys at a secret frat party instead of a posh event. Ruby rolled her eyes. Boys masquerading as men, she thought, half listening as they traded stories about their sexual exploits that were clearly too far-fetched to be believed.

'Wait till you hear this one,' one of them said in a low voice. 'The other night Michael picked up this girl and get this—' the wag paused for effect '—he says he kissed her and didn't even realise it was his ex until she slapped his face and told him they'd broken up six months earlier. Apparently she'd changed her hairstyle and got implants.'

'God, I wish I had his life,' a nasally voice whined. 'He's an animal.'

Before she could give them a snarky look another voice interceded, a deep, velvet-coated voice she'd listened to all evening one long-ago night.

'He's an idiot,' he said. 'No man forgets a woman he's kissed. At least he doesn't if he has any integrity.'

Ruby's heartbeat doubled and her skin turned pasty beneath her heavy make-up. *It couldn't be him. It just couldn't!*

'What can I get you, ma'am?'

Startled by the question, Ruby stared blankly at the bartender.

'To drink,' he offered, gesturing to the vast array of colourful bottles on the marble shelf behind him.

'Sorry.' Ruby cleared her throat and forced herself to relax. 'I'll have…' She frowned, trying to remember what Molly and her friend had asked for. 'I'll have two Cosmopolitans and a white wine.'

'Riesling? Chardonnay? Chab—?'

'Whatever's strongest,' Ruby cut in. *And make it fast, please.* Her palms were sweaty and she clasped them together, willing herself not to turn around to check who owned that all too sexy voice.

Fortunately she didn't hear it again and when the bartender finally returned with her order she threw him a relieved smile and grabbed her drinks.

Keeping her head down, she turned and would have run smack into the side of one of the men if a masculine hand hadn't shot out in front of her. Liquid sloshed over the side of one of the glasses and her eyes flew upwards to meet concerned brown ones.

Bedroom brown eyes with thick, dark lashes.

Her pulse raced erratically. It was the man in the bronzed mask. The tall one with the impossibly wide shoulders and long legs. The one who had saved the woman from being eaten by the swan. The one with the chocolate-brown hair brushed back in mussed waves just like Sam's, and the impossibly kissable mouth perfectly positioned in a smoothly chiselled jaw. Also, just like Sam's.

A shaft of liquid heat detonated low in her pelvis, sending plumes of sensation outwards just as it had done in that trendy pub two years ago. Just as it had done at Miller's wedding one year ago.

It's not him, she assured herself. *It's not him. It's not—*

'Sorry about that.' A hint of a lazy smile played at the edges of his mouth. 'My fool acquaintance wasn't watching where he was going.'

Ruby froze, her IQ falling by a hundred points. The man who—*please, God*—couldn't be Sam Ventura cocked his head with bemused candour at her stultifying silence, his gaze falling to her lips before drifting lower and stopping on the drinks she was gripping precariously in front of her. 'You need a hand carrying those?' His dark gaze returned to hers. 'I'd be more than happy to assist.'

Mentally berating her stunned-mullet act, Ruby kicked her brain into gear and clamped her lips together. This was *not* Sam Ventura. He was just a very good-looking, powerfully built replica who *seemed* very much like Sam Ventura.

'Thanks, but no, thanks,' she bit out in a low tone. 'Believe it or not, I don't need a man to make my life perfect.'

And why on earth had she said that?

Grimly aware that she had silenced them all, she turned her back on the little group and willed her jelly legs to hold her upright as she hurried back to Molly.

Well, well, well, if he hadn't just been put in his place by the very beautiful, and very cool Ruby Clarkson, Sam mused, watching as she disappeared into the crowd as if the hounds of hell were after her. Because, as surprising as it was to run into her so soon, it *was* her; there wasn't a shred of doubt in his mind.

A fiery spark of heat ignited inside him as he noted the graceful, swan-like neck and hourglass figure in the lavender gown. Obviously she hadn't recognised him and that was a little...*disappointing*?

Two years ago he'd kissed her and felt as if he were standing on a tight wire being swung from side to side without a safety net to catch him. One year ago he'd wanted to repeat the experience and could have sworn she did too, and now she passed him by as if he was what? Nobody special? An irritant, even?

Ignoring the four bozos he hadn't liked in high school and liked even less now, Sam grabbed his beer and headed into the party as the men behind him laughed uproariously at another lewd story that was as likely to be true as Sam suggesting that his father had put him first as a boy. Pure fantasy.

Shoving that thought back where it belonged, he took a pull of his beer.

Had Ruby really not recognised him?

The thought was like a burr in his side as he caught sight of lavender silk from across the room.

Not her, he realised as the woman lowered her hand-held mask to speak to her companion. His heartbeat steadied and he frowned as he realised that it had sped up in the first place. He wasn't here to hit on anyone. He certainly wasn't here to hit on Miller's off-limits friend. Yet he couldn't deny that his senses were instantly charged at having seen

Ruby again so unexpectedly. Which had answered one of his earlier questions—no, the attraction he felt for her hadn't lessened. Not even a little.

But what about for her?

He stood and watched the lively partygoers for a moment, wondering if he should prop up the bar for a bit, or head to a quieter corner until enough time had passed that he could leave. Or maybe he should hunt Ruby Clarkson down and wait for her to recognise him.

And what then? a little voice taunted. *Surely you're not thinking of finishing that thing you started two years ago?*

Sam tilted the bottle of beer to his lips and took another long, fortifying pull.

Was he thinking that?

He couldn't deny that the idea still held some appeal. More than some appeal, if he was being honest. Ruby Clarkson was a beautiful woman. What man wouldn't want a long-legged, curvaceous honey-blonde woman spread out beneath him, naked and wanting in his bed, those glorious green eyes glazed over with desire, her lips plump and wet from his kisses, her creamy thighs parted for his possession?

Sam's body hardened at the images rampaging through his head and softly cursed his wayward libido. No doubt she'd be great in bed. Great in *his* bed.

And there was that niggly note of ownership that had given him such pause two years ago. The caveman element that only she drew out of him. He didn't like it. He didn't like how effortlessly she drew him to her, or how often he thought about her. He certainly didn't like how possessive he felt about her. Would one night with her in his bed solve that? Would one night rid him of the powerful pull she seemed to have over him or would it only make it worse?

Sam's brooding gaze noticed a hint of lavender drift through the crowd towards the dance floor. Well, there was really only one way to test that theory, wasn't there? Not that he intended to take her to his bed tonight. He wasn't that desperate. But he could have a little fun with her, couldn't he? A little innocent fun just until she recognised him. A smile curved the edges of his lips as he set off towards the dance floor. How long would it take her? One minute? Two?

Suddenly the evening looked a whole lot more interesting than it had half an hour ago.

CHAPTER TWO

'I DON'T SEE anyone who looks like a pirate,' Ruby said as she stood on tiptoe to see over the packed dance floor. 'Are you sure that director is even here?'

'Katy said he was.' Molly's lips tightened determinedly. 'I have to find him. I'm psyched up to approach him, and who knows when I'll get another chance like this? It's not as if I can get a ticket to these kinds of events just by clicking my fingers.'

Ruby gave her sister a faint smile and tried not to look over her shoulder again for the man in the bronzed mask. She'd felt his eyes on her as she'd all but run from the bar, and she'd been so sure he'd follow her she'd been on tenterhooks ever since.

'I think that's him,' Molly whispered, low-level excitement running through her voice.

Ruby's stomach lurched. Then she realised that Molly hadn't meant Sam Ventura's doppelganger and told herself to stop fretting and breathe. It wasn't Sam. Sam was in LA.

She glanced at the man Molly was so set on meeting and did a double take. The director-slash-pirate was big, blonde and fierce-looking. 'Are you sure that's him?'

'Almost certain. Let's dance so I can get closer.'

'You dance, I'll hold the drinks,' Ruby said, taking Molly's half empty cocktail glass and nodding towards the dance floor. The sooner Molly introduced herself to the famous director and begged for an audition for a part in his next movie, the sooner they could leave. 'Time to walk the gangplank, my lovely.'

Molly surreptitiously smoothed a palm down the side of her gown. 'I thought you said this was a hare-brained idea?'

It was a hare-brained idea but seeing her confident, madcap sister suddenly nervous, Ruby softened. 'It's a great idea. He's going to love you. Just remember: no public sex.'

Molly smiled at that. 'Of course not. Sex can come after I've won an Oscar for starring in his film and if we fall madly in love with each other.' She straightened her shoulders and set her jaw determinedly. 'You sure you won't dance with me?'

'In this dress?' Ruby glanced down at her enhanced cleavage. 'Not a chance.'

Molly scowled. 'You're no fun.'

'I know. I work really hard at it.'

Laughing, Molly blew out a nervous breath and headed into the fray. Ruby sometimes envied her little sister her ability to put herself 'out there' like that. Ruby could do it for her clients but when it came to pursuing something for herself…well, she wasn't that brave, and knowing that was one of her greatest strengths.

Sipping her drink while she held Molly's, she savoured the crisp lightness of the wine, almost forgetting about the man in the bronzed mask until she glanced up and found him prowling towards her, a sexy grin on his face.

Instantly her breath backed up in her lungs and her pulse took off like a rocket. As if he sensed her response, a heated gleam entered his eyes, darkening them from chocolate to mink. 'When you ordered those drinks I didn't realise you intended to drink them all by yourself,' he said, his intimate tone and soft laugh inviting her to play along with his charming joke.

A shiver snaked down Ruby's spine at the sound of that deep, velvety chuckle. Oh, this guy was smooth. Dangerously smooth. He was also most definitely Sam Ventura. What was the point in trying to deny it any longer?

'Another lame pick-up line,' she said with cool derision. 'How very original of you.'

Instead of taking her comment as the put-down it was meant to be, Sam seemed highly amused by it. 'I didn't realise I'd delivered a first one.' His eyes glowed from behind his mask as he grinned down at her. 'Now, if I told you that you had the kind of smile that could stop a man at fifty paces…that would be a lame pick-up line.' His smile widened. 'It would also be true.'

Ruby blinked up at him, feeling a distinct height disadvantage without her usual four-inch heels on her feet, her gown not long enough to accommodate them. His tone implied that he thought she was a stranger, but how was that possible? She had recognised him straight away—would recognise him blindfolded in a dark room just by the prickling awareness he set off inside her.

She didn't know whether to be insulted or glad that he hadn't recognised her in turn. Maybe both. It only seemed to confirm that the mutual connection she had believed was special between them the night they met hadn't been special or mutual at all.

Something inside her chest plummeted just a little more. Her pride, no doubt, because what woman's pride wouldn't be dented when a man who had kissed her as if he couldn't get enough of her now had no clue as to who she was just because of a silly costume?

Dismayed to have her worst fears confirmed, Ruby deliberately disguised her voice with a smoky edge. Let him try and pick her up, she thought with rising irritation. Let him try and use all his sophisticated charm on her and have her turn him down this time. She'd like nothing better than to see him dig a hole for himself and then reveal her identity at the last minute. It was no less than he deserved for not calling her when he'd promised that he would.

And, yes, she knew she needed to get over that but she really hated when a man said one thing and did another. She'd experienced the disappointment of being let down by her father too often as a young girl to put up with it in her adult life.

'Great outfit by the way. I'm thinking you're—'

'Don't say Little Bo Peep,' she warned menacingly.

Sam laughed softly. 'If you were Little Bo Peep you'd have a staff. And sheep. Which might not work with those ducks earlier.'

'Swans.'

'Ducks, swans...feathered fowl who belong in a pond, not at a masquerade party.' His dark eyes glittered with lazy male appreciation as he gazed at her. 'Not without a mask at least.'

Ruby's lips twitched and she quickly sipped the last of her wine. She was not going to find him charming this time around. She was not going to feel breathless with awareness, or tingly with anticipation. She was not going to remember the gentle way he had tucked a strand of her hair behind her ear before he'd said goodnight to her two years ago. Or the way he had looked at her as if she amazed him. It had made him impossible to forget. Impossible to get over. And thinking like that was just asking for trouble.

'So no nursery-rhyme jokes and no lame pick-up lines,' he agreed. 'Want to dance instead?'

'I don't dance with strangers,' she mumbled, glancing furtively towards the dance floor in the hope that Molly was ready to go home. Of course, Molly was nowhere to be seen.

'Stranger?' He cocked his head. 'That's easy enough to remedy—'

'No!' Her eyes widened on his. She wasn't ready to reveal who she was to him. She didn't want to have an awkward conversation about the past. It wasn't as if they were friends. They weren't, and they never would be. Better if he just left her alone and was none the wiser as to who he was trying to hit on. 'No names.'

'No names?' He gave her a curious look.

'Half the fun of wearing a mask is being anonymous. Don't you agree?'

'This is my first masked ball. I'm new to the etiquette.'

'Then allow me to educate you.' Her voice dropped further to a husky purr. 'Names aren't necessary.'

'Is that right?' The lights dimmed around them as the music turned soft and sensual. Ruby's heart thumped against her ribcage. She really needed to get away from him and the way he made her feel.

'So if you don't want to dance and you don't want to trade names—' his gaze drifted to her lips like a feather-light caress '—what do you want to do?'

Kiss you, she thought, her body already responding to his lingering look. *I want to kiss you and never stop.*

'One dance.' He gave her a slow smile as if he

knew the appalling direction in which her mind had just taken her. 'I'm harmless, I promise.'

'I'll call you tomorrow, I promise.'

The last thing Ruby wanted was to find herself in Sam's arms again but he was so smooth he'd divested her of the two glasses she'd been clutching like a lifeline and had her there before she had time to blink.

Which only made her angry. What was it about this man that eroded her natural born caution? She didn't want this and she certainly didn't want him. Only, she knew she was lying to herself. There was something about Sam Ventura that got to her every single time and try as she might she couldn't seem to do anything about it.

She risked a glance up into his eyes to find him watching her closely. Did she feel familiar in his arms? She was shorter without her heels on but...

Oh, get over yourself, Ruby Jane. He doesn't know who you are so forget it. Have a laugh.

But she couldn't have a laugh, not with his heat surrounding her and setting her pulse racing, not with his face so close to hers she could see the beginnings of his beard coming in, and not with his scent, spicy and masculine with a hint of sandalwood, short-circuiting her brain.

All she could do was remember the feel of his skin beneath her fingertips, slightly rough, his lips warm and firm against her own. It was like being sent back in time. She wanted to feel those lips again.

She wanted to feel the power of his need again, his hunger for her. She'd never felt like that in a man's arms before and it was nothing short of addictive.

No man forgets a woman he's kissed before. At least he doesn't if he has any integrity.

Did he remember kissing her? Would it come back to him if she was to reach up and kiss him now?

Inwardly shocked to realise where her thoughts were leading her, Ruby jerked back. Kissing Sam Ventura was the last thing she should be thinking of doing. This man was dangerous to her equilibrium. She knew it as surely as she knew her own name.

'You okay, angel?' He drew her closer as she stumbled, bending to murmur in her ear. Ruby's breath caught as his warm breath skittered across the sensitive skin of her neck. That name—he'd called her angel two years ago as well…

Shaking off the unwanted memory, she firmed her resolve against his effect on her.

'No, I'm not okay,' she said, making her first sane decision of the night and stepping out of his arms to push blindly through the throng of oblivious party-goers as she rushed from the room.

A stone terrace loomed in front of her, showcasing a captivating view of the harbour beyond, and Ruby headed for it, swiftly moving some distance down a narrow terraced walkway lined with fairy lights that wound around the side of the house.

'Wait.'

Unaware that Sam had followed her, but not surprised, she stopped, the throb of the music just a low beat now they were outside.

'What happened back there?' His concerned gaze caught hers, his eyes scanning her face. He was so close to her she could feel the heat and energy from his body permeating her own.

Panic was what had happened back there. Jumbled senses and racing pulses was what had happened. Need and want…

'Listen,' he began, reaching for his mask. 'I think it's time we—'

'No!' Ruby startled him into silence when she grabbed for his arm and prevented him from unhooking his mask. She couldn't think of anything worse than him unmasking himself now because he'd expect her to do the same. Which would put her in the position of explaining why she had acted the way she had. It would mean she would have to explain how she'd felt so overwhelmed by the heat of his body, his touch on her waist, his breath against her skin, that she'd run. Explain how in that moment she had wanted more of it. More of him.

'Hey…' he murmured softly, accurately reading her inner distress, his fingers gentle as he touched her chin. 'Look at me.'

She did, the low light of the garden casting shadows across his strong jaw and carved lips, his dark hair falling forward over his mask.

He was so beautiful. So masculine. The bronze

of the mask giving him an otherworldly appearance that only added to his appeal.

Ruby's breathing altered, becoming choppy as they stared at each other. She tried to shake her head to clear her senses but his fingers prevented her from breaking eye contact with him. She irrationally felt light-headed, drunk on the clean, intoxicating scent of musk and man. Then his other hand sought the nape of her neck and she didn't know if he leaned down further or she stretched upwards but suddenly his lips were on hers, warm and firm and utterly compelling.

Wide-eyed, she met his stunned gaze and then she couldn't help herself: she lowered her eyelids and opened her mouth. She heard a deep groan rumble out of his chest as he felt her submit to the inevitable and he slanted his lips more fully across hers to deepen the kiss. It burned through her like liquid fire, drugging her, consuming her, triggering an avalanche of need deep inside she was powerless to resist.

A faint voice in her head warned her that this was a mistake, that if she played with fire she'd get burned. She heard it and accepted it, but stronger than that was this fierce, unbidden need for this moment to continue, for this pleasure never to end. She didn't know if it was the intimacy of the night, the mask hiding her identity from him or the fact that she'd denied herself any form of sensual pleasure for so long, but she knew she was as lost to his touch as she had been two years ago. Maybe more so.

His lips moved over hers, sure and confident, her senses so attuned to the feel of him that she felt when he would have pulled back from her.

'Don't,' she murmured softly, her arms around his neck. 'Please, don't stop.'

Sam groaned and complied with Ruby's request even though logic and instinct told him to—*for God's sake, man*—rein it in. It had been like this with her two years ago. Intensely intimate, sinfully erotic. Just the touch of her mouth against his was enough to have him losing his head. Now, holding her like this, feeling her unguarded response to him was sheer, unadulterated torture.

His arms banded around her, urging her closer, the soft, desperate whimpers coming from the back of her throat driving him to move them both further into the shadows cast by a small, cut-away corner of the building.

Her arms tightened around his neck and Sam ran his hands down over the boning of her gown. She arched against him, her breasts rising and falling above the low-cut neckline, threatening to spill out. Breasts he'd longed to see, longed to taste.

Telling himself that he'd stop this lunacy in one more moment, he slid his hand along the slender curve of her arm and shoulder and down to cup her rounded flesh in the palm of his hand.

Her breath caught inside her chest and she arched higher against him. Sam sensed the need in her, felt it in his own blood, and seared an urgent path of heated kisses down the long line of her neck. Her head fell back as a shiver went through her, her body leaning more heavily against his. He braced his arm across her lower back, his feverish eyes taking in the creamy skin of her décolletage, pearl-white in the ribbons of moonlight that breached the overhanging trees.

Heat and fire coursed a dangerous path inside him, burning up all rational thought as sensation overwhelmed him. A vessel blew its horn somewhere out on the harbour, someone laughed gaily as they jumped into the pool. Sam barely heard a thing, the sounds receding beneath the heaviness of his own thundering heartbeat.

Ruby's lips were soft and yielding beneath his, feeding off his with the same violent hunger that turned him harder than stone. He shifted closer, bringing their bodies into perfect alignment, taking her soft moan deep into his mouth.

'Damn, you taste good,' he murmured, his lips moving to the sensitive skin beneath her ear. She writhed in his arms, her greedy hands growing more restless and bold as they ran over his shoulders and into his hair.

His mask was in the way and he was about to wrench it off when she pushed his jacket back and he had to shuck out of it. Then her sharp little nails raked his skin as she tugged his shirt out of the waistband of his trousers. Hunger bit deep and he hauled her upwards, his mouth returning to hers with a primal need.

Sam had been with many women in his thirty-one years, pleasured more than he could remember, and he knew he was a good, giving lover, but this... touching Ruby, hearing her soft cries of pleasure as he discovered what pleased her, was a sensual delight he hadn't reckoned on. He was completely at the mercy of his senses and he not only wanted to take everything she had to offer but he was also prepared to give her everything in return.

'More,' she begged, leaning into him and kneading his back muscles like a hungry kitten might a downy quilt. Sam swore under his breath and gave her what she wanted, urging her back against the vine-clad wall of the house and putting his hands all over her. Moulding her hips and her ribs, the soft swell of her round breasts. Breasts he had to see. Had to touch.

Somewhere in the back of his head an alarm bell was ringing but it was competing with the soft sounds of their mutual need, and really, what was one more minute of madness?

Lifting her so they were at eye level, Sam leaned forward and kissed the rounded swells of her breasts and then forced the top of her gown to give so that one pert nipple popped free.

'I want to taste you.' His voice sounded guttural with urgency and he didn't wait for her response, lowering his head and taking the tight pink bud deep into his mouth. He flicked her aroused flesh with his tongue, relishing the soft keening sounds that told him she was as lost to this madness as he was.

'Oh, God.' She arched into his hold, her fingers threaded through his hair. 'I need you,' she said on a rushed breath, her fingers fumbling as they moved to his belt buckle.

Knowing he should stop, but unable to, Sam gathered the yards of fabric between them and skimmed his hands along her thighs. A tiny, flimsy scrap of silk was all that separated him from paradise and with one tug it gave, falling to the ground between them.

A low growl radiated up from his chest as his fingers found her soft and wet. He wanted to drop to his knees and taste the sweet honey coating his fingers but she was already rising against him.

'More, please, I want more.'

He caught her mouth and propped her against the wall. Part of his brain tried to kick in, tried to remind him that he was a civilised man who did not have sex with women outside at important parties, but the hot throb of her body shredded his sanity and made a mockery of his self-control.

All he could think about was replacing his fingers with his throbbing shaft and making her his. Something she obviously wanted just as badly because she was tearing at the zip on his trousers and then he was free and she was open and ready, her thighs cradling his hips intimately against his body.

That first contact of his flesh against hers gave him pause because he didn't have a condom on him. Cursing himself for his lack of preparation he was about to tell her when her lips cruised down the line of his neck and she bit the tendon between his neck and shoulder.

A shiver went through him, a groan dragged from deep inside as he forgot all about reason and responsibility and gave into a need that was stronger than he was, entering her on one hard, perfect thrust.

She was so tight. So snug… His body tensed as he fought to control his most basic urge to possess her.

'Relax for me, angel, and this will go easier.'

Sweat beaded his forehead but before he could fully process that there was something untutored to her movements Ruby angled her body upwards and took him deeper, scattering his thoughts.

'Slowly,' he urged, holding her hips steady between his hands. 'That's it, let me all the way in.' He groaned as her silken muscles rippled around him, holding him tight. Careful not to crush her, Sam placed a hand against the wall to support them both, his legs shaking as he strove to hold off his own release until he felt hers first.

'Oh, God.' She clutched at him, her little nails scoring the nape of his neck. 'I…I…' Her body squeezed his, small lake-like ripples pulling him in deeper and harder as her body sought, and found, the ultimate release.

As soon as he felt her peak Sam let go, moving inside her with controlled power as his own climax raced through him like never before.

He didn't know how long they stayed like that, their bodies joined in the most fundamental way, their lungs heaving. Gradually he became aware of their surroundings: the way his shirt stuck to the damp skin on his back, a cicada making a racket in a nearby bush, the low throb of the music coming from far inside the house.

He lifted his head from where it was buried against Ruby's sweetly curved neck, his legs so weak he had to fight to hold them both upright. He felt her shift against him and the enormity of what they had just done, of how out of control he had been, hit him hard.

He cursed softly and lowered her to the ground. He didn't regret many things in his life but taking Ruby with all the finesse of an untried schoolboy just might turn out to be one of them. He wanted nothing more than to wrap her up and take her home so that he could do that all over again. In a bed this time. 'Are you okay?' he prompted softly, knowing that he felt as dazed as she looked.

'Water.' She blinked up at him, her mask slightly askew from his fingers. He wanted to rip it off, yank off the wig and let all her long, golden hair tumble free. 'I'm so thirsty,' she croaked. 'Do you mind?'

Sam raked his hair back from his forehead. No, of course he didn't mind getting her a glass of water, but first he wanted to apologise, tell her he hadn't meant for things to go that far. At least not outdoors, at a party of all places! He cursed inwardly again. 'Sure, water.' The apology could wait. 'Just…stay put until I get back.' Hesitating, he glanced down at her, his brows pulling together as he took in her trembling mouth. 'You're sure you're okay?'

She nodded, fussing with her voluminous skirts so that she wouldn't have to look at him.

Leaving his jacket on the ground Sam strode back the way they had come, blinking as he rounded a corner and his eyes met the brighter lights of the terrace, small clusters of partygoers thankfully ignoring him as he stalked inside.

Quickly fetching a glass of water, he rehearsed a short speech in his head on his way back, trying to come up with some plausible explanation for what had just happened between them, only to find the place he had left her empty.

Worried, he spun around, searching out the shadowy garden for any sign of lavender silk. It took him a full minute to realise that she wasn't there. Then another to realise that she'd done a runner. Worry gave way to guilt that he'd taken things so far with her, and finally to fury that she wasn't still waiting where he'd left her.

Did she do this kind of thing all the time? Pick up a man, have unforgettable sex with him and then ditch him when his back was turned? Was that why she had insisted that they keep things anonymous?

Jaw clenched, Sam yanked off his mask and tossed it to the ground. He couldn't quite bring himself to believe that she had used him in such a way, but if she thought he wouldn't pursue it she couldn't be more wrong.

CHAPTER THREE

'RUBES, IF YOU don't hurry up you'll miss yoga,' Molly called from outside her bedroom door.

Still in bed, Ruby rolled over and wondered if she could pretend to be asleep. Considering that she hadn't slept all night, she felt heavy enough to pass it off as real.

'Ruby?' Molly opened her door and poked her head inside. 'Are you ill?'

Yes, she was. She had just told a man she didn't even like that she *needed* him the night before. While they'd been having sex. Outside. At a party. The very thing she had warned her younger sister not to do!

Sex?

Was that really all it had been? It felt more like a cataclysmic event that had changed everything for ever from this point on. Certainly it had been the most erotically charged event of her life. In fact, before last night she had never understood how anyone could get so carried away with a man that they didn't stop when their common sense asserted itself. Unfortunately if her common sense had asserted itself she hadn't heard it.

It was the way he had looked at her and touched her that was the problem. He made her feel so special and so hot she literally lost her mind in his presence. Not that she *was* special. How could she be when he hadn't even known her name?

'Ruby?'

Or that she'd been a virgin? Although there was a moment of hesitation where she'd wondered if he had guessed at her inexperience. It had been cowardly, but the fear that he would question her about that, coupled with his soft curse of regret afterwards, had been the reason she had run when he'd gone to get her water. Not her finest moment, for sure, but when faced with the alternative of unmasking herself and saying 'Hi, it's me, Ruby. Great sex, by the way, thanks for the initiation' she'd chosen the easier, less confronting option. And didn't regret it for a second!

The fact that Sam Ventura would never know she had been the one he'd had hot vertical sex with was the one saving grace that made her confident she could face the day.

'Ruby, you're scaring me.'

Ruby glanced up to find Molly's worried brows knitted together. 'What? Sorry.' She forced her mind back to the present.

'You don't look well. What happened last night?'

'Nothing. I'm fine.' Ruby pinned a smile on her

face, hoping that one day it would be true. 'Give me five minutes and I'll join you for yoga.'

'You sure you're up to it?'

No. But it was better than lying around in bed thinking about how stunningly erotic sex with Sam had been and how she was unlikely ever to experience anything like that again.

'I'm sure.'

Her sister looked unconvinced. 'I've made coffee, so hurry.'

As soon as Molly closed the door Ruby dashed out of bed. She knew from texting her sister last night that she'd met with the director and after some convincing he'd agreed to give her a call to set up an audition. Thankfully, Molly hadn't cared that Ruby had left the party without her, happy to continue on with the thespian crowd after successfully completing her quest.

And yoga was the best thing that she could do. It helped re-centre her enough to keep her mind off her excruciatingly bad decision on Friday night and stopped her from conjuring up future disasters as a result of her uncharacteristic indiscretion. Future disasters like the fact that she'd had sex for the first time in her life with a man who didn't even know her name. Like the fact that if Sam had still worked for the same firm as her, and ever found out it was her and told someone, the gossip would be all over chambers before she'd finished swiping her key card in the office lift.

Fortunately he lived in LA, so he was as likely to find out it was her he'd had sex with as she was of flying to the moon.

Small mercies, she conceded as she ducked out of the Monday morning summer rain and into the coffee shop she regularly haunted before work. She'd almost convinced herself that she'd pushed the whole Friday night affair from her mind when a tall, broad-shouldered man entered the coffee shop behind her, shaking the morning drizzle out of his dark hair.

With her heart in her mouth Ruby waited for him to turn towards her and as he did she felt a sense of unreality come over her when she realised it wasn't Sam.

The man gave her a small smile as she continued to stare, and Ruby made an apologetic face and swung back to the barista fixing her coffee. She felt jumpy all of a sudden and that just wouldn't do. She wasn't going to run into Sam in the middle of George Street. If anything she'd call Miller later in the day, find out how long Sam was in town and then avoid him for the duration.

If only the sex hadn't been quite so good.

Not good. More like amazing, mind-blowing, *incredible*. Other phrases that came to mind were: over, never to be repeated, and *stop thinking about it!*

Determined to listen to her saner side, she nodded at the dark-haired man whose attention she still inadvertently had as she strode out of the coffee shop and crossed the road to her office. The sooner she started work and felt normal again, the better.

'Hey, Ruby.' Veronica, her upbeat secretary, called out as she held the lift door open. 'How was the Herzog gig Friday night? Did you meet anyone nice?'

Why was everyone so interested in her love life all of a sudden? 'The Herzog party was fabulous.' She knew if she didn't show the right amount of enthusiasm that Veronica would prod her for more information. 'How was your weekend?'

'Took the kids to the zoo and saw the baby panda. So cute. So was there anyone interesting at the party? A celebrity or two?'

'Not that I noticed. We were in masks, don't forget, so that made it harder to recognise anyone.' Thank God. 'Why are you getting off at the third floor?' Their office was on the fourth.

'There's a meeting in the big conference room. Didn't you get the memo? Mr Kent Senior is making an announcement. We all received emails about it on Friday night.'

Ruby had come straight from court on Friday night and even though she remembered seeing the internal memo in her inbox she had forgotten to read it as she was rushing to get ready for the party. 'When is it?'

'Now,' Veronica said. 'Aren't you coming?'

'Of course.' Ruby stepped out of the lift, mentally reorganising her morning while juggling the file she'd been reading, her leather briefcase, hot coffee and her phone.

'Want me to hold something for you?'

Ruby shook her head. 'I'm good. Any idea what the meeting's about?'

'Rumour has it that our firm is about to merge with a big-shot outfit from the States.'

Ruby paused with her coffee halfway to her lips. 'Sorry?'

'But Bridget from IT said it was about Mr Kent Senior finally retiring and Drew taking over as managing partner.'

Ruby released a relieved breath. That sounded more like it but she wished Mr Kent could have just sent the information in the memo. She had a full day already mapped out and fitting in a Monday morning conference would be like trying to thread yachting rope through a sewing needle.

Seeing her expression, Veronica gave her an encouraging smile. 'It's supposed to be brief.'

'It's always supposed to be brief,' Ruby grouched before letting her bad mood wash away. So she'd be inconvenienced for half an hour. She loved her job and if Mr Kent wanted to go out with a bang then she wouldn't begrudge him his moment. He'd built a wonderful firm and deserved to have everyone acknowledge the work he'd done.

Manoeuvring herself into the overcrowded conference room, she greeted various co-workers with a smile as she moved towards the back. There was a real buzz in the air and Ruby craned her neck to get a glimpse over the sea of heads as to who was seated at the front of the room, only catching a glimpse of her boss, Drew Kent. Drew was a great boss: level-headed and fair-minded even when he didn't completely agree with some of the cases she took on, like her current one. It made her try that much harder to prove her worth, which she supposed was one of the reasons she'd done so well in the firm since she'd started working here twenty months ago.

'Everyone, if I could have your attention, please.'

Ruby sipped her coffee as Drew took the floor.

'It is with great pleasure, and much relief, that I announce the retirement of my father, who we all thought was not going to leave the building unless it was feet first. Fortunately my mother has convinced him that there is more to life than the law, even though we all know that isn't true.' A cluster of moans interspersed with chuckles filled the cramped space, making Ruby smile.

He said a few more words about his father's being an inspiration and introduced him to rousing applause. Mr Kent Senior then good-naturedly harangued his son in return and suggested that the only reason he'd finally agreed to leave the firm in Drew's capable hands was that someone highly regarded had agreed to merge his firm with theirs and help Drew run the show. Surprised murmurs filtered around her like a colony of bats preparing to take to the skies at dusk.

Ruby's ears pricked as she waited to hear who the newcomer was, and when she heard the name Ventura International her stomach plummeted to the ground faster than a lead ball dropped from the Sydney Tower.

'I'm sure you'll all join me in showing your appreciation for the fact that we've lured one of the most esteemed names in law back from the United States and doubled our legal reach by merging two great firms together.'

Although the crowd clapped heartily, Ruby stayed stock-still. This couldn't be happening. It just couldn't. She forced herself to oxygenate her lungs but it felt as if she'd never done it before and it was a skill she had yet to master. The coffee she'd consumed churned in her stomach and she had to swallow hard to keep it down. How was this possible? It was a nightmare. It was a disaster. It was…there were no words to describe how she felt other than numb. Totally and completely numb.

She heard Sam say a few words about how much he was looking forward to working with everyone and what it meant for him to be there but all Ruby heard was *'I want to taste you.'*

Oh, God, she was going to be sick.

Suddenly everyone around her was forming a line in order to congratulate the new managing partner and Ruby's stomach did another weird flip. She had to calm down. She had to pull herself together. She had to find a bathroom before she lost her breakfast all over the carpet.

'Can you believe we're going to be working out of Wellington Towers from tomorrow onwards?' Veronica said with barely concealed excitement. 'The foyer alone is as big as an aircraft hanger and apparently it has one-hundred-and-eighty-degree views of the harbour. No more cramped offices and narrow hallways. We're going to be working in the lap of luxury. I can catch the ferry to work now rather than taking the smelly old bus!'

Right now Ruby would believe that the sky was falling in if Veronica told her. 'Wellington Towers?' Her brows lowered in confusion. She'd clearly missed that part of Sam's speech.

'Apparently Sam owns it. Five floors of office space were cleared out over the weekend to make way for the merger. A lot of the hardware and case-sensitive info has already been moved out too, so it's just our personal stuff that has to be—Ruby, are you okay? You look white as a sheet!'

Ruby glanced at Veronica and gripped her forearm. 'Actually, I feel terrible. Just...' She looked around wildly as she felt herself being inched forward in the line to greet their new boss. 'I'll see you in my office.'

Veronica frowned. 'Sure, sure. Want me to give Mr Ventura your apologies?'

'No.' Ruby squeezed her arm. *Lord, no.* 'Just don't

mention me *at all*.' Because she was going to have to resign, so why bother mentioning her name?

Five minutes of deep yoga breathing later she felt no better, but at least she was no longer thinking about resigning. She loved her job and there was no way she was going to have her career sidelined by a man. She'd made that vow a long time ago.

And why would he sideline her career anyway? He didn't know she was the woman he'd had sex with at the party on Friday night. As far as Sam was concerned, she was Miller's best friend he had shared a few kisses with a couple of years ago and that was it. No big deal. Nothing to get bent out of shape about. And perhaps he'd been too drunk to remember kissing her that night two years ago…she certainly hoped he was too drunk to remember having sex with her at a party three nights ago.

Nearly knocking over one of the paralegals as she exited the bathroom, she apologised profusely over her shoulder and stepped straight into the path of the long, self-assured strides of her current boss and…*her new boss*.

Heart hammering, Ruby first met blue eyes and then molten brown, her breath backing up in her lungs, her brain automatically registering how big and devastatingly good-looking Sam Ventura was *sans* mask. He was a couple of inches taller than Drew, his white shirt with the blue stripe perfectly complementing his olive skin tone, his navy-blue suit jacket stretched perfectly across his broad shoulders.

Her gaze lingered on his clean-shaven jaw and sensual mouth. He had pleasured her so thoroughly on Friday night her body immediately felt hot all over. Hot and weak. Especially when she remembered the way his mouth had felt on her breast, the way he had used his teeth and his tongue to torture her with mindless pleasure.

Coffee surged out of the spout of her to-go cup and dribbled over her fingers. Squeaking in dismay, she brought her hand to her mouth to capture the drops before they hit the carpet and nearly tipped the whole contents out instead.

Sam reached forward to pluck the cup out of her nerveless fingers while Drew handed her a handkerchief from his breast pocket.

'Ruby? *Hell.* Are you burnt?' Drew asked, concern lacing his voice.

'No,' Ruby croaked. *Just embarrassed.* 'It was cold.'

She kept her focus on Drew, knowing she would turn stop sign-red if she looked at Sam.

'Okay, well, I'm glad we caught you. I didn't see you in the conference room at the meet and greet,' Drew said.

'I was there,' she assured him. 'I uh…had to duck out.'

'So you know Sam and I are sharing the managing-partner role?'

Ruby's lips stretched into a tight smile. She'd missed that bit of the speech as well. 'Great. Congratulations.' She cast a quick glance at Sam to include him in her felicitations, only to find him studying her far too intently.

Ordering herself to *act normal,* she gritted her teeth and broadened her smile to make it more genuine. 'Welcome to the team.' A team that would soon be less one lawyer. Her. Because her first instinct had been spot-on: she would have to resign. There was no way she could see him in the office every day and remember everything they had done in Technicolor detail and then actually work for him in any sort of professional capacity.

'Thanks.' Sam's deep voice reverberated through her whole body, tightening every nerve ending to an excruciatingly fine point. 'I'm pleased to be here.'

She nodded, wondering if he had known she worked at the firm before Friday night…which was completely irrelevant because he didn't know he'd even been with her on Friday night. *The cad!*

'It's good we ran into you,' Drew said, cutting into her increasingly irrational thoughts. 'I was just bringing Sam to your office.'

Ruby tried not to show her alarm. 'You were?'

'Yes. With Mandy about to go into labour any day now, Sam has agreed to oversee the Star Burger case and I'd like you to bring him up to speed. Once this thing hits the media it's going to be bigger than *Ben Hur*, and I'd feel much better having a senior partner on board.'

As much as Ruby wanted to ease Drew's mind

right before his first child was born, she had this case well in hand. 'Really, I have everything under control,' she advised him, hoping she sounded cool instead of defensive.

'Your last update said you were planning to put a political bigwig on the stand. This thing is getting huge, Ruby.'

'I'm not just planning it,' she stated crisply. 'I intend to do it.' She didn't mean to bristle but she knew Drew had been dubious about her taking this pro bono case in the first place, and there was no way she was going to pull her punches now or, heaven forbid, drop the case altogether. Star Burger was an immensely popular chain of restaurants throughout Australia. The owner, Carter Jones, had franchised his business but had neglected to put in ethical standards to protect his employees. As a result everything from discrimination to racism and underpayment ran rampant throughout the organisation, and Ruby aimed to prove that it started at the top down.

Winning would not only mean that her badly treated clients were paid the money owed to them, it would also give a group of young people who were typically vulnerable in the community a voice they'd never had before. 'And it already is huge.'

'Which is why Sam needs to help you out,' Drew said, 'he has experience with cases like this.' He looked from Sam to her. 'Plus he said you already know each other.'

He had? Ruby swallowed. 'Only because my best friend married his brother. We don't actually *know* know each other.' Okay, so that time she had definitely sounded defensive; she knew it and steadfastly refused to look at Sam.

'I can take it from here, Drew,' Sam assured the other man calmly. 'You still want this?' He held the cup of cold coffee up to her.

'No. But it's a reusable cup, so you can't throw it away.'

'Fine.' He held on to it for her. 'You'll have to lead the way. I have no idea where your office is.'

Unable to come up with a plausible reason to defer their meeting, she gave him a tight smile. At least he didn't know what had transpired between them on Friday night. It was a small comfort, considering she did know and it was all she could think about, but she clung on to it anyway.

Cool as a cucumber, Sam thought, watching the sway of Ruby's body as she marched ahead of him, her pencil skirt lovingly outlining the sweet curves of her bottom and long legs that ended in skyscraper heels. This was the Ruby he'd met two years ago in the bar, all sharp edges and take-charge attitude wrapped in a glossy, unruffled package.

Or so she would have him believe. Because she wasn't entirely unruffled if her inability to maintain eye contact with him was any indication. That could be shock, of course, at having him turn up at her workplace. He was a little in shock himself. He hadn't known where Ruby worked before today and there was no way she could have known he was about to merge his firm with Kent's.

They had deliberately kept the merger quiet so as not to tip off the markets until it was a fait accompli. But this development, having Ruby as an employee, certainly threw a spanner in the works. He'd planned to get her phone number off Miller this week and call her up. Demand an explanation as to her actions last Friday night and then tell her what he thought about them. Tell her that next time she had sex with a man, she needed to wait around so that he could make sure she was okay and see her home.

Given that she was treating him like a veritable stranger right now, she probably wouldn't have responded to his call very positively. But they weren't strangers at all. They were lovers. Well, maybe not *lovers*. A lover didn't run out on a man after she'd sent him to heaven and back, did she?

Sam frowned, his earlier fury with her returning full force. Did Ruby even know it was he who had been inside her delicious body not fifty-eight hours ago? He who had made her come so hard that she had clung to him like a baby koala about to fall out of a tree? The thought that maybe she *hadn't* known had crossed his mind more than once over the weekend, but he'd immediately dismissed the notion. She'd known it was him. He was sure of it.

But what if she hadn't? What if he'd been little

more than a random hook-up she'd used to scratch an itch? Sam felt a deep growl rumble inside his chest. A part of him didn't like to think that was all it had been for her, which was slightly irrational because wasn't that all it had been for him?

Her stride slowed as she reached a secretarial desk, her face only slightly softening as she listened to the woman seated behind it. He studied Ruby's profile. Her thick, straight hair was bound tightly at the base of her skull and he wanted to unwind it and mess up each blonde strand until it sifted like silk through his fingers.

'If you'll give me a minute,' she said coolly, turning to look at him. 'I need to take an important call before our meeting.'

Sam planted his hands on his hips as he regarded her. Was this a power play? Make him cool his heels while he had to wait for her?

'Fine,' he finally said, attempting to give her the benefit of the doubt.

'Would you like a coffee while you wait, Mr Ventura?'

'Sam,' he automatically corrected the secretary. 'And no. I'm fully caffeinated. Thanks.'

'No worries.' She smiled widely at him and he could see she wanted to say more but he paced around the small space like a caged tiger, his mind boiling over with the possibility that Ruby had no clue as to who he was other than her best friend's brother-in-law.

'You can send Mr Ventura in now, Ronnie.' Ruby's voice sounded over the intercom, raising his hackles. Mr Ventura, was it?

Of course, idiot, you're in the office, not a bar.

Fine. He'd be calm and professional in return. Let her know he preferred first names in the office just as Drew did and then he'd ask her if she was okay. And perhaps why she'd sent him on a fool's errand on Friday night and then run away from him.

'I'd like to get something straight,' she said, seated behind her desk like a queen attempting to exert control over a particularly unruly minion. 'I know how busy you must be with the merger, and the move to new office space this afternoon, so I don't want you to feel that you have to involve yourself in the Star Burger case. I have an incredible team working with me and we really do have everything well in hand.'

The woman had spunk; he'd give her that. 'And hello to you too, Ruby. It's good to see you again,' Sam drawled, somehow managing to hold his fast-rising irritation in check.

She had, he noticed with some satisfaction, the good grace to blush. 'It's ah…nice to see you too.'

Like hell it was, he thought, refusing to sit down opposite her like the good boy she expected him to be. Instead he took his time studying her office as if he were truly interested.

'I just don't want you to think that I need your assistance right now,' she continued as the silence lengthened between them. 'I know you must be incredibly busy.'

'So you said.' He picked up a colourful paper-weight from her bookcase and tossed it into the air. 'Nice piece. Who gave it to you?'

'My mother.' She moistened her cherry-red lips, a signature look of hers if he remembered correctly. 'After I made Senior Associate.'

'That's right.' He looked across at her. 'Drew said you're very good at your job.'

'Extremely good,' she corrected, more defensive now than uncertain. 'I've worked hard to get where I am at Kent's.'

'I didn't say you hadn't.'

'I know, but some people assume it's because of Drew's affirmative action strategy and—oh, never mind.'

'Relax, Ruby,' he said, finally dropping into the club chair opposite her desk now that he had control of the conversation. And her. 'This isn't a job interview. I wasn't having a go at your position in the firm. I'm sure you've earned it.'

Her eyes narrowed. 'Yes, I have. Now, what is it you need from me exactly?' *Before you hurry up and leave*, her tone implied.

'That depends.' Sam quirked a brow. 'What are you offering? Exactly?'

She took a deep breath and he took more pleasure than he should in knowing that he'd succeeded in riling her. 'Mr Ventura—'

'Sam,' he interrupted. 'You can start by calling me Sam and then you can continue by telling me why you're so prickly.'

'I'm not prickly.'

'As a porcupine being poked with a stick.' He relaxed back in the seat. 'Unless this is your usual working demeanour, and if it is then I might start questioning how you got so far so fast after all.'

'I apologise,' she said stiffly, smart enough not to take his bait again. 'I didn't mean to sound rude. I'm still getting my head around today's announcement about the merger and the changes that will bring.'

'Understandable. Now, tell me what the phone call was about.'

'Phone call?'

'The one you had to take while you left me outside, cooling my heels.'

'I didn't do that.'

'You did, but I'm not going to quibble over it. Did the call have anything to do with the Star Burger case?'

She frowned, clearly not wanting to share any information with him. 'Yes. But, as I said, I know you must have a hundred things on your plate, so you don't need to worry about this case right now.'

Sam looked at her, taking in the smooth line of her jaw and the challenging glint in her green eyes. Of course he had to worry about the case. Star Burger Restaurants was owned by one of the wealthiest men in Australia, a known pig of a man, who habitually treated people badly. Four months ago a group of young migrant workers had formed an alliance and decided to do something about their shocking working conditions and had approached legal aid for help. Legal aid had directed them to Ruby's desk and the case had grown exponentially until they now had a class action on their hands. It would be a landmark case in Australia if they won.

But he'd get to that later. First up he wanted to find out what Ruby's deal was and whether it had anything to do with their tryst on Friday night. 'So your resistance to having me work on this case is not because you're worried that Drew thinks you can't handle it, but for my benefit—is that right?'

'I can handle the case just fine.' She frowned darkly. 'And I think it's overkill to have you stepping in at this point, especially if you're under the impression that I *need* you. I mean, that I need your *help* or...anything.'

'Pity that's not your call to make, isn't it?'

His tone was cool and challenging and Ruby had no comeback because they both knew he was right: it wasn't her call to make.

'This is a David and Goliath case, Ruby,' he continued softly. 'Once it hits the media, Carter Jones will go after your clients' reputations with a vengeance and you'll need to be ready.'

'I know all this. I know we're the underdogs.' Concern pleated her brow. 'It's an impossible case to win, everybody says so, but no matter what you say to me, I have no intention of dropping it.'

'Dropping it?' Where had that come from?

'Yes. I know Drew was concerned about Kent's taking it on in the first place, and I know he's worried about how big it's going to get, but it's too important to drop now. We've come too far.'

Sam frowned. 'Have I asked you to drop it?'

'No.' Her chin came up and she unconsciously moistened her lips again. 'Are you going to?'

'No. But I know Carter Jones and I know how ruthless he can be. If this case goes to court it could severely damage his standing in the community, not to mention Star Burger Restaurant's profit margin. He won't allow that at any cost.'

'Then he should have made sure he took better care of his employees,' she said with a spiritedness Sam couldn't help but admire. 'Because this case is going all the way, Sam. These boys need justice and I intend to see that they have it.'

'Well said, and you'll get no argument about that from me. But surely you can see how having a lead partner on the case transmits a level of gravitas to the proceedings that might not otherwise be there.'

'You mean it will intimidate the opposition to have Sam Ventura on the case?'

Sam inclined his head. 'I have a reputation for winning, but then so do you. I think Drew's idea is that together we'll make a formidable team.'

'And if I disagree?' she asked archly.

Sam regarded the jut of her chin and stiff back and decided to push her some more. 'Another decision that isn't yours to make.'

She made a low sound in the base of her throat, her eyes shooting daggers at him. 'Fine. Do whatever you like. It's not as if I can stop you from coming in and taking over, is it?'

Sam ran a frustrated hand through his hair. 'Ruby, this isn't about your ability to run the case, or us dropping it, and it's not about me coming in and taking over. But this case is a class action. You're going to need senior counsel on it whether you like it or not.'

She gave a heavy sigh, her shoulders slumping a little. 'It's not a class action any more. Another client has dropped out, leaving only six.'

'Six?' That shocked him. 'You started with nineteen.'

'I know. Carter Jones and his cronies have already started intimidating them. The boys don't understand the system and therefore they don't trust it. But the remaining six want to go ahead and I intend to stand by them.'

Sam drummed his fingers on the arm of his chair. Six wasn't going to be enough to defeat Jones. 'Set up a meeting with all nineteen,' he said decisively. 'I'll speak with them.'

'All nineteen?' Ruby looked at him dubiously. 'I'm not sure that's a good idea. I don't want the remaining six to pull out as well.'

Sam raised a brow. 'You don't trust me very much, do you, Ruby?'

'It's not a question of trust,' she said, her eyes not meeting his. 'I don't want you wasting your time if you don't have to.'

'Now it's my turn to get something straight with you,' he began quietly. 'I'm a big boy, Ruby, and believe it or not I'm fully able to decide what is, and what isn't, a waste of my time. Understand?'

'Of course.'

Sam watched her even white teeth sink into her bottom lip and felt his body react. He could see that she still wasn't happy about him stepping in and he now knew it wasn't entirely due to her ego being pricked. Which left only one other issue outstanding between them.

'Now is that it? Or is there another reason you don't want to work with me?'

Harried green eyes cut to his. 'I didn't say I didn't want to work with you.' She let out a breath and, to her credit, tried to smile. 'You're Miller's brother-in-law. Why wouldn't I want to work with you?'

'Perhaps because we have more history between us than my brother and his wife,' he said equally as coolly. 'Perhaps because I've had my mouth on yours.'

Not to mention on your neck, your hair, your breasts.

A momentary flicker of panic darkened her emerald eyes before she shut it down, reaching for her water glass, her hand trembling only slightly as she brought it to her lips. 'That was two years ago and has nothing to do with any of this.'

'Doesn't it?'

'Of course not. It was an impulsive, late-night thing on both our behalves and it meant nothing.'

Sam didn't like hearing her say it had meant nothing to her, even though he had told himself the same thing at the time. But what happened two years ago was chicken feed compared to what had happened between them on Friday night.

'Since we haven't seen each other since then,' she continued doggedly, 'we should…we should…' She shrugged one slender shoulder. 'Just forget it ever happened.'

Sam stared at her for a beat. 'But we have seen each other since then, Ruby.' His ego scratched at the surface of his skin, goading him to push her. 'At Miller and Tino's wedding nearly a year ago? Don't you remember?'

'Of course.' Relief was stamped into each breathless word. 'How could I forget? It was a beautiful night.'

'How's the banker, by the way?'

'Banker?' A small frown notched between her brows. 'Oh, you mean Chester. He's a stockbroker.'

'I didn't ask *what* he was. I asked *how* he was.'

'He's good. I think he's good. Anyway, moving on…'

Unbelievable, he thought with growing incredulity. She was not going to acknowledge Friday night at all. And that left him in a bit of a quandary because not only did he want to mention it, but he also wanted to repeat it.

Not a good idea, Samuel. You're her boss now.

'Maybe I'm not ready to move on,' he found himself saying, regardless of what he'd just told himself. 'Maybe I want to explore things some more?'

'Explore things?' He'd admire her poise more if that pulse at the base of her throat wasn't fluttering like a trapped bird trying to get away from a hungry cat. 'Why would you want to explore anything about Chester Harris?'

Sam shook his head and told himself to back off. Whether she knew he had been the one she had been urging to take her on Friday night or not didn't matter. He had to let that go. Stop obsessing over it. If he wasn't careful he'd make this whole thing more important than it needed to be and that should have been more than enough to cool his interest in her.

More than enough to stop him from wanting to slip beneath the polished, professional facade this woman wore as convincingly as she had worn the black lace mask on Friday night and find out if the fire that had burned so brightly between them was for him and him alone.

'Don't stop. Please, don't stop.'

His jaw flexed. Because, as irrational as it might be, he wanted her to admit that she had known exactly who she had welcomed into her stunning body, and he wanted to have her there again. Hot and wet just for him.

But he couldn't do that. She worked for him. Even more reason he should use his brain and let this thing between them die a natural death.

Which meant no more leading questions about what that kiss had meant to her two years ago, and no informing her that he knew she was the woman he had held against a wall and buried himself deep inside until he'd seen stars last Friday night.

Watching her now, he told himself to take a very large step backwards. His feelings—whatever they were—for Ruby Clarkson didn't belong in the office. Or in his head.

He'd been back in the country for three days, he was hardly looking for any kind of relationship, and on top of that Miller would probably deliver his balls on a plate if he started something with her best friend, only to drop her a week later.

A best friend who looks like she would rather stick hot needles in her eyes than start something with you, Ventura.

'Sam?'

Her confused voice broke into his thoughts. 'What?'

She frowned across at him. 'I asked if you agree with me.'

No, dammit, he didn't agree with her. Especially when he'd been so lost in thought he hadn't even heard her. 'Agree with what?' he barked, coming to a stop in front of her desk, his fingers digging into his hipbones.

'That we should forget all past—' she cleared her throat, moving a document from one side of her desk to the other '—*interactions* between us if we're going to work together.'

When he didn't immediately respond she lifted her gaze to his, one eyebrow raised in query as if they were discussing the merits of cucumber sandwiches. Her cool regard was like waving a red rag at a particularly irate bull and Sam ignored all his earlier good advice to himself to back off and went straight for her jugular. 'Friday night,' he said with a savage smile. 'Did you enjoy yourself on Friday night?'

A swift tide of emotion darkened her eyes and then she blinked and it was gone. When she spoke her voice was as steady as an ocean liner, her brow puckered with just the right amount of confusion as to appear genuine. 'Why would you ask me about Friday night?'

God, she would make a formidable opponent in court, he thought with unwilling admiration, his ego slightly mollified by the overactive pulse still thrumming at the base of her neck.

'No reason.' He forced a lazy smile to his lips. 'Miller mentioned that you work long hours. Even weekends. I wouldn't want you to burn yourself out.'

'Oh.' She glanced over his shoulder at the door as if she wanted it to open magically and suck him outside. 'I'm not nearing burnout. Thank you for asking.'

She rubbed the outer edges of her left eye as if to control a twitch. Sam's smile grew. Oh, she knew all right. She knew he had been the man who had been inside her at the Herzogs' party, the man who had pleasured her so deeply, so thoroughly, so *intimately* he'd had to hold her upright immediately afterwards so she didn't fall over. He was dead sure of it now. And damn, if that didn't ease the choke hold she had on his unaccountably fragile ego.

'My pleasure,' he purred, buttoning his jacket and willing to back off now. 'Set up that meeting with every one of our Star Burger clients. And Ruby?' He stopped at her door and smiled at the wary expression on her face. 'Thank you for your time. It was very enlightening.'

CHAPTER FOUR

RUBY SAGGED IN her seat the moment Sam closed her office door behind him.

Good lord, she was never going to be able to work with him. He was too big and too dangerous to her equilibrium, sucking all the air out of the room until she could barely breathe.

The way he had looked at her, all hot and intense...it was all she could do to hold herself aloof. And when he had asked about last Friday night...her eyes narrowed as she recalled his bland expression. She'd almost been certain he'd been toying with her, but he was a master when it came to inscrutability.

Even so, there was no way he could know that he'd been with her at the Herzog party. No one had known her there, as far as she was aware. The only way he would know it was her was if she told him. Which she wasn't about to do. Ever.

'Here are some boxes,' Veronica said, carrying in two cardboard flat-packs she immediately set about constructing on Ruby's desk. 'I know you have a lot to do today so I'll take care of the packing up. Just remember tomorrow when you finish in court to head to the new office building. With the amount of manpower Sam has provided we'll definitely be in by then. And we're on the executive floor.' She waggled her brows. 'I'm going to do my best to get us a view of the harbour. How *was* your meeting with His Hotness before? He looked a lot happier when he left than when he was standing around waiting for you.'

'His Hotness?'

'That's what a few of the girls have already nicknamed him. I'm married, but I wouldn't mind locking lips with him just once in this lifetime. I'm sure my husband would forgive me.'

Veronica grinned and Ruby tried to grin back. 'He's unlikely to remember you afterwards,' she said with enough bite to have Veronica looking at her strangely.

'What does that mean?'

'Nothing.' Ruby pushed back from her desk and started shoving things into the first box. 'Ignore me. I'm upset that another client has opted out from the Star Burger case. I have to set up an appointment for all of them to meet. I think Sam has some idea that he can convince them to re-commit to the case.'

'Maybe he can. He's awfully compelling.'

About to tell Veronica she didn't really want to hear how 'compelling' their new boss was, she stopped when there was a knock at her door.

'Werner meeting about to start in five, Rubes.' Grant Campbell, a rising-star associate in the firm, poked his head through the door. 'We're in conference room four.'

'On my way,' she said, grabbing her laptop and accidentally upending five case files in the process.

She glanced at Veronica. 'Ever get the feeling you should have stayed in bed some days?'

'All the time,' Veronica quipped.

And that was pretty much Ruby's day, chasing her tail and trying to keep up with work until she fell into bed that night so tired she didn't even think about Sam the whole night. Or mostly.

By Wednesday morning she felt marginally more in control, though she used that term loosely because she could already feel her nerves buzzing around inside as if she were high on caffeine. Which she wasn't because she hadn't even had time for a coffee so far this morning.

She stared at the view of the Opera House outside her new office window. Veronica had done well, nabbing a great space for them in the impressive tower. The Manly ferry pulled up to the wharf, unloading a small colony of workers and a few eager tourists onto the fastidiously tidy Circular Quay area far below.

She was just wondering if she had time to work out how to use the state-of-the-art coffee machine in the kitchen when her phone buzzed. She glanced down to find a text from Grant regarding the Star Burger case. Apparently some of the nineteen plaintiffs had arrived and were drinking cola and eating cake in the conference room.

Sending him a quick thank-you in reply, she rolled her chair back and scooped up her file notes on each one of her clients along with her laptop.

Even though she had emailed Sam the information yesterday morning, he had asked that she stop by his office an hour before the meeting to go over their strategy together. It was the last thing she wanted to do, given that she'd steadfastly avoided any contact with him the last two days, but it had to be done.

Today she wouldn't be able to hide in her office if she thought she heard him outside her door, or turn the other way when he was coming towards her down the hallway, her insides jittery as she waited for him to call out to her and ask her to stop. Her fixation on his whereabouts in the office was making her crazy and, what was worse, interfering with her usually fanatical concentration levels.

Channelling all things serene, she pushed her feet back into her favourite don't-mess-with-me stiletto heels and checked her immaculate red lipstick before making her way to the end of the hall, knocking sharply on Sam's office door.

Sam uncoiled from behind his glass desk as she entered his lair, an unreadable expression on his face. She noted his impressive physique in his pale blue shirt, royal blue tie and charcoal suit trousers. He looked like the uber-successful lawyer that he was and she knew her clients would be incredibly intimidated by his powerful aura. Couldn't the man tone it down just a little bit?

'Why the frown?' he asked, his voice gravelly as if he hadn't spoken for a while.

Deep breaths, she told herself. He might live up to his new 'hot' label but she was a professional. Plus, she'd been there, done that, and now she was blushing and he was looking at her in that intense, curious way of his. How he didn't know that they had been as close as two people could ever be was beyond her, and it was definitely absurd for her to be thinking like that when she was *extremely happy* that he didn't know it was her at the masquerade ball.

Not that she should be thinking about *that* night at all. This case was incredibly important for her and she genuinely cared about her clients, who she had rapidly come to think of as 'her boys'.

Boys who were only teenagers and new to the country, a couple of them barely speaking English but all of them hungry to learn and to find a place to belong where their safety wasn't at risk every other minute of the day. Star Burger Restaurants should have provided them with a place of employment that espoused the egalitarianism that most Australians liked to be known for. It hadn't, and it was Ruby's job to prove that management had not only known how her clients had been mistreated, but also that the rot in the organisation was filtered from the highest level down.

Would Sam take the case as seriously as she did? Or would he see it as a vehicle to showcase his prowess in the courtroom? And why did that matter if he helped them win?

'Stop biting on your lip,' he rasped, 'and tell me why you're frowning.'

Ruby released her newly tortured flesh, hoping she hadn't eaten her lipstick off in the process. 'I'm frowning,' she said softly, 'because I'm concerned about our meeting today. Some of these kids went through a traumatic experience working for the Star Burger chain and it's been really hard gaining their trust. I don't think going over things yet again is going to help.'

Sam sat down on one of the white leather sofas set in an L-shape looking out over the cloudless blue sky of a summer's day. 'They'll have to repeat their stories if it goes to court.'

'Which is why most of them pulled out.'

'No. Most of them pulled out because Carter Jones started a smear campaign against them. We need to get those clients to re-engage in the case if we want to win and you know it. Come. Sit down.'

'They don't trust the system,' she told him, reluctantly doing as he'd bid and taking a seat on the spare sofa adjacent to his. 'And why should they? It hasn't done them any favours so far.'

'It will after we win their case.'

Ruby's brows drew down. 'Just don't push them too much, okay? They don't know you from Adam.'

Sam cocked his head, his gaze raking her face to

the point of discomfort. 'You care about these boys almost more than you care about winning, don't you?'

'I care about doing what my client wants me to do,' she said, pushing her hair back behind her ears. She didn't want Sam to think she brought excessive emotion to her cases because it was one thing to be passionate about work, but quite another to be so involved you stopped being impartial and became ineffective.

'I have been around the block once or twice, Ruby—I do know what I'm doing.' He gave her an all-encompassing look. 'Is that the only thing making you so jittery right now?'

Ruby's head reared back. 'First you say I'm prickly, now you say I'm jittery. I'm neither,' she said hotly, her stomach doing a somersault and making a mockery of her words. Lord, if he could see through her so easily, she was toast.

'Good. Then help me work out the best strategy to get the full nineteen boys back on board. If we want to beat Jones we're going to need them to at least agree to show up in the courtroom, even if they have no intention of taking the stand. It will give our current clients a confidence boost and hopefully worry the hell out of Jones.'

Ruby unclamped her lips and found herself envying Sam his ability to remain so composed while she felt as if her insides were getting ready to audition for the lead role in one of Molly's musicals. But then he wasn't constantly distracted by flashbacks as to how it had felt to have her hands all over his body on Friday night. How it had felt to have his hands all over hers. And why couldn't she manage to put that behind her? It had been five days already.

'I know you care about these boys, Ruby,' he said softly. 'You're not as hard-nosed as you'd like me to believe.'

Ruby opened her file notes and lifted her chin. 'I'm exactly as hard-nosed as I want you to believe.'

Sam shook his head and moved from his sofa to hers, his powerful thigh brushing against hers as he settled too closely beside her. Fire shot through her at the slight touch and she surreptitiously adjusted her position further along the settee, ignoring his sidelong glance.

'Ready?' She arched a brow in question.

'Always.' He took the first file from her and Ruby exhaled as his agile brain switched from her to work, forcing her own to follow suit.

Three hours later Ruby was quietly impressed with the way Sam had approached the case. He did know his stuff and had gone out of his way to put the boys at ease, asking insightful questions and never pushing in a way that might be construed as threatening or manipulative.

Now, with the meeting about to finish up, she couldn't wait to get out of there. A whole morning of being this close—and this aware—of her new boss had her nerves strung tight. And some sixth sense told her that Sam knew exactly how she was feeling.

It seemed that she only had to take a breath and he glanced her way. It was unnerving. *He* was unnerving. Why on earth had she become so carried away on Friday night that she'd ignored every cautionary note in her head that screamed *Stop!* and instead had listened to the racy one that had moaned *More*?

'Thank you all for coming today. I know it wasn't that convenient but I truly believe if we stand together we can win this case for you,' Sam began. 'I also think that it's vital that we win this case for you. Your lives mean something here, they mean something to us, but you need to stand up and believe that too if you want to see justice done for each and every one of you, now and in the future.' A couple of the boys fist-pumped the air in agreement, while others shifted uneasily in their seats, none unmoved by Sam's passionate discourse. 'I know you have to think about everything that was said today but if you could email Ruby by the end of the week with your decision as to how you want to proceed we would greatly appreciate it.'

Relieved to have the meeting over with, Ruby stood up hastily and shook each one of the boys' hand as they headed for the door. A couple of them gave her a hug and she returned it enthusiastically. Grant stopped beside her, giving her a *that went well* look, but before she could head out with him Sam asked her to stay behind in a voice that brooked no argument.

Glancing back, Ruby found that Sam was scrawling notes in a file and not even looking at her. Grant raised a brow at her in question. Sam's directive had come across more like a command but the last thing she wanted to do was extend the meeting. Her nerves were shot.

'Actually, I have another meeting I need to prepare for,' she said politely. 'Can it wait?'

Sam frowned as he glanced up at her. 'No. It can't.'

Ruby moistened her lips. 'Perhaps an email, then?'

Grant coughed into his hand and quickly gathered up his laptop and file notes as he caught Sam's darkening expression. 'I'll leave you to it.'

Aware that she had probably overstepped the lines of professional decorum with that last suggestion, she stood tensely waiting for Sam to finish making his notes.

And waited.

And waited.

Finally he leaned back in his chair and looked at her, his long, thick lashes concealing his expression from her. 'Mind telling me what that was all about?'

'What?' she asked, stalling for time.

'Your desire to scramble out of here as quickly as possible.'

'I don't scramble,' she said indignantly.

'You also don't have a meeting to get to. I checked with your secretary earlier because I wanted you to stay back and go over a few key points with me.'

Irritated at his high-handedness, Ruby bristled. 'How dare you go over my head and ask Veronica about my movements? If you want to know my schedule you can ask me.'

'I didn't go over your head. You were busy talking and I saw no point in interrupting you for something so small.'

His raised brow told her she was overreacting—and not only that but it was also a reminder that he was her boss and could do what he damned well pleased—so she sucked in a deep breath and forced her lips to curve upwards. 'Fine. What key points?'

'Thabo and Jeremiah were particularly nervous today and their stories didn't seem to stack up with their original depositions. Why is that?'

'Jeremiah has a minor learning disability. It's one of the reasons he was ridiculed in the workplace. He's been on medication ever since to manage his anxiety and I think it messes with his memory.'

'We should strike him from the client list, then.'

'We can't. He deserves to be heard as much as anyone else.'

'I didn't say he didn't. But we have to be practical. He'll get compensation like the others, but he shouldn't be subjected to the witness box if this goes to court. It could make his health worse.'

'If?'

'Don't get your back up again. I very much doubt Carter Jones will let it go all the way.'

'But it has to. How else will our clients receive full validation for how they were mistreated?'

'Money will go some way to appease them.'

'That's not true,' she fumed. 'You know they're not motivated by money. They want justice.'

'They'll get justice. Now tell me about Thabo.'

'I have a feeling Thabo is standing in for someone else who doesn't want to come forward.' She tucked a strand of hair behind her ear and noticed his eyes follow the movement. 'I think it might be a woman. If you haven't noticed there are no women on the case because they're too frightened to come forward. I think that's why Thabo is defensive.'

'Which also makes him a weak link.' Sam frowned. 'But the women need to be as equally compensated as the men. Can you find out if we can get any of them to come on board?'

'Of course.' She cleared her throat, suddenly aware that she'd moved closer to him during their discussion. 'Is that all?'

'You tell me?' His rough tone did nothing to placate her frazzled nerves.

'I have nothing else to tell you,' she said carefully, unnerved by the sexual tension that suddenly permeated the air between them.

'I think you do.'

The way he looked at her tangled her insides up and twisted her emotions into a tight ball. He was so attractive with his shirtsleeves rolled up and the top button of his shirt loosened, the curl of chest hair overlapping the button screaming that he was all male. Something she already knew by heart.

'And I think it's past time we addressed the elephant in the room, don't you?'

'Elephant?' She had a sick feeling she knew where this was heading. 'There is no elephant.'

'Then why are you so keen to avoid me every chance you get?'

Ruby hunted around for an explanation and went with what was uppermost in her mind. 'If you must know, I don't think we can work very well together.'

'Why not?'

Now, there was a question she had no intention of answering. 'The why, or why not, isn't important.' She hated that she felt so flustered and defensive and that only made her feel more so. 'I respect you as a fellow lawyer and as my boss, I just don't respect...' Her eyes shot to his as she realised what she'd been about to say.

'You just don't respect what, Ruby?' His voice was predator-soft. 'You don't respect me as a man. Is that what you stopped yourself from saying?'

Yes, it had been because how could she respect a man who had sex with random women whose names he didn't even know? 'I didn't say that—you did. But I don't see any point in letting this get personal between us. It will only make things harder.'

Sam gave a short, harsh laugh. 'It's a bit late for that, don't you think, *angel*?' The tone of his voice had all the hairs on the back of her neck standing on end. 'Things are about as personal as they can get between us, I'd say.'

Ruby tried not to overreact to the word 'angel',

fighting to remain calm. 'If you're talking about how I wanted to leave the meeting, I—'

'I'm not talking about that.' He dismissed with a careless flick of his wrist, his gaze disturbingly direct. 'I'm talking about Friday night.'

He waited a beat but Ruby found her tongue frozen to the roof of her mouth.

'Last Friday night, to be exact.' When she remained mute he gave her a sardonic smile that only elevated his good looks. 'You know... You and me. Sizzling-hot sex outside at the Herzog party. Or are you going to tell me it wasn't you in the lavender silk dress and black lace mask?'

Oh, God, she had been wrong.

He knew. He *knew*! The words reverberated inside her head, a stinging heat singing along her cheekbones as if she were being pricked by a thousand tiny hot needles.

Their gazes clashed and held and Ruby couldn't look away from his gorgeous brown eyes to save herself.

'I can see you're still going to try and deny it,' he said, the savage note in his voice letting her know that he was far from impressed with her. 'Which is a little disappointing, to say the least.'

'I'm not going to deny it,' she said with asperity, mortification setting in as she recalled how she had begged him for more that night.

'Well, that's a start,' he grated, his gaze penetrating every one of her natural defences in a way no man ever had before.

What was it about Sam that made him so lethally attractive to her? It just wasn't fair.

'A start to what?' she asked, recognising for the first time that he was truly annoyed, but at a loss as to know why he would be. She hadn't demanded anything from him, or called his phone off the hook like a love-struck fool. Shouldn't he be rejoicing about that instead of scowling at her?

'To you being honest. I did wonder if you were going to try and blame the alcohol. Maybe claim that you'd had so much to drink that you didn't know what you were doing. That you didn't know *who* you were doing it with.'

If only I could! But what did he want her to say? That she found him so completely and utterly irresistible that she hadn't been able to stop? That she had wondered what it would be like to be intimate with him for so long that when it finally happened she hadn't *wanted* to stop? 'I knew what I was doing.' She lifted her chin, determined that he would never guess how deeply she was affected by the intimacies they had shared—or how much she had enjoyed it. 'And I'm not ashamed of what happened.'

A scowl darkened his face. 'Were you ever going to mention it?'

'No,' she answered after a brief pause, her heart pounding like a jackhammer behind her breastbone.

'You had an itch and I scratched it.' His lips twisted into a cool smile. 'Is that it?'

Taken aback by the force of that comment, Ruby scowled. 'There's no need to sound so crass.' Was that the way it had been for him? She felt a little sick at the thought, immediately reminded of the soft curse of regret he'd made before he'd set her on her feet. 'But yes, I suppose you could put it that way. What's your excuse? Or don't you need one? You're a man, I was an available woman. Isn't that the way the story goes?'

Dead silence followed her accusation and when he spoke his voice was grim. 'That would imply that I got more out of our lovemaking than you did. Which is not my recollection of events.'

Embarrassment at just how much she had begged him to keep going burned a hot trail down her throat. 'Oh, come on, Sam. Lovemaking? Let's at least call it what it was.'

'By all means.' A muscle flexed in his jaw. 'Enlighten me.'

Ruby gripped her laptop tighter. 'It was sex. Great sex, by the way. Ten out of ten to you, but it was still just sex.'

'It was nowhere near ten out of ten,' he corrected her.

Well, sorry. Hurt cut across raw nerves as if he'd just lashed her with a whip.

His dark eyes held hers as if he knew exactly where her mind had taken her. 'Ten out of ten would have meant we were in a bed, naked, and we had all night together.'

'Oh.'

Well, then.

Not sure where to look, she watched him covetously as he moved to the window and stared outside. Without his eyes on her, Ruby breathed a little more easily, but her reprieve was short-lived as he swung back to face her.

'There's something I want to know.'

Ruby held her breath at the serious note in his voice. 'What?'

'Was that your first time?'

Caught completely off guard by the question she blinked at him. Had it been so obvious?

A soft curse rent the air.

Crimson-faced, she turned to leave.

'I didn't use protection.'

His words landed between them like boulders off the side of a mountain, staying her. 'I'm on the pill.'

His eyes narrowed as he looked at her. 'Why is a virgin on the pill?'

'Because I was planning to have sex with someone that night, and you were the lucky recipient. Why do you care?'

'Because I was worried I might have made you pregnant,' he argued. 'An unwanted pregnancy is the last thing either one of us needs right now.'

The image of Sam Ventura's baby growing inside her womb did weird things to Ruby's equilibrium. Not wanting to consider that any of those things were bad, she shook her head. 'Rest assured, I'm not pregnant. No need to worry.'

An emotionally charged beat passed between them and all Ruby could think about was the way his sexy mouth had felt on hers and how much she wanted it there again.

Deep down, she rued the day she had approached Sam in that bar two years ago. It had set off a series of wants and needs inside of her that she could only ever imagine him fulfilling. She hated the romantic feelings he had once inspired in her and she was very afraid that if she gave herself to Sam—truly gave herself to him—he would take more than she would want to give, knocking down every one of the barriers she had built up specifically to keep him out.

'I apologise,' he said, a measure of self-disgust running through his voice. 'It shouldn't have happened.'

Did he mean they shouldn't have had sex? Somehow that only made her feel worse. She really didn't need more proof as to how divergent their experience of that night had been. She'd already seen the regret on his face; she didn't need to see it again.

'Please don't.' She put her hand up as if to ward him off but he was still on the other side of the room. 'We're both adults and it was my decision as well.'

'I wasn't apologising for the sex, Ruby.' His brown eyes glittered dangerously into hers. 'I'm apologising for not protecting you. For being...rough.'

'You weren't rough,' she assured him huskily.

His eyes pierced hers. 'I should have realised that you weren't experienced.'

'Why should you?'

'Because it's a man's job to take care of a woman in that situation.'

'I disagree. This is the twenty-first century. Women are emancipated, in case you didn't realise.'

A muscle ticked in his jaw. 'Emancipation had little to do with Friday night,' he growled. 'But let's just say it's not the way I usually behave with a woman.'

At the mention of his other women Ruby expelled a rushed breath. This was information she didn't want inside her head. Ever. 'Look, can we just not discuss this any more?' Surely there was a much more important and safer topic for them to discuss. Or they could both just leave the room and pretend this conversation had never happened at all. 'Don't you have a meeting to go to or a new client to woo?'

Ignoring her question, he came around the table until he was no more than two feet from her. She nearly took a step back but caught herself just in time.

'Why did you run away afterwards?'

Startled by his question, she met his gaze. 'Sorry?'

'It's a simple question, Ruby. I want to know why you left before I returned with your water.' His bronzed throat worked as he swallowed. 'Did I scare you somehow?'

Being so close to him now, she couldn't avoid the sensation of heat and male power emanating from him. There was also impatience, as if he wanted to close the gap between them and take her into his arms again. Or was that just her who wanted that to happen?

Jarred by the unexpected vision of how he would

look naked, and desperate to close down this attraction any way she knew how, Ruby shook her head. 'I was fine. I just didn't see the point in hanging around.' Not to mention that she'd been terrified at how easily he had made her feel so much, so quickly. Terrified at how easily she had given in to the attraction between them. It had made her feel weak and powerless; two states she had often seen her mother fall into with the men in her life. 'I mean, it wasn't as if either of us was looking for a repeat performance, was it?'

Sam's jaw clenched. 'You have no idea what I wanted, but be that as it may, it would have been polite for you to have been there when I returned. I didn't know if I'd hurt you in some way.'

'You didn't hurt me, Sam,' she said on a rush, memories of the pleasure he had given her making her knees tremble. 'And you didn't scare me. I was just… I wanted to put the whole incident behind me as soon as possible.'

'Incident? It wasn't a car accident,' he bit out.

'I know that! Really, I'd rather not talk about it, if it's all the same to you.'

'I can see that.' She didn't like the derisive glint in his eyes, or the way he stepped forward. 'But I very much doubt that you've been able to put the whole *incident* behind you.'

Heat flamed through her. It was pretty hard to put something behind you that came back in full, cinematic glory every night when you tried to go to sleep.

Not to mention those times it was standing right in front of you. Like now.

'God, you're arrogant.' Against her better judgment she took a step towards him. 'But *be that as it may*, we work together now. You're my boss.'

Sam frowned. 'I didn't know that on Friday night. It wasn't as if Drew sent me a list of Kent's employees to pore over.'

'So if you'd known I would be working for you on Friday night then it wouldn't have happened?' she challenged.

'Believe it or not, Ruby, I didn't mean for things to go as far as they did.'

'So you're blaming me for the fact that they did!'

'No.' He braced his hands on his hips, scowling down at her. 'Dammit, would you stop being such a little hothead? I'm telling you that I never mix business with pleasure, and I usually take a woman out to dinner before I sleep with her.'

'We didn't sleep together, Sam.' A charged silence followed her statement and Ruby suspected Sam was remembering exactly what they had done, just as she was.

'A technicality,' he said shortly.

'And a moot point, since it's never going to happen again. And, for the record, I don't mix business with pleasure, either.'

Fortunately, she wouldn't have to think about that for much longer she decided as a conversation she had overheard between her colleagues the day before came back to her. An interoffice transfer was not something she'd ever considered in the past but it might be exactly what she needed. And sure, it might be considered a little impulsive and she'd never been the impulsive one in her family before, but, compared to having sex with a man she hardly knew outside at a party, a work transfer was minuscule. 'Nor do I want to start a relationship with any man any time soon. In case you're wondering.'

'Career first? Is that it, Ruby?'

'Always,' she responded briskly.

'Well, I don't recall saying anything about a relationship either,' he mocked.

'Sorry,' she said tightly. 'I meant to say fling, or affair, or whatever you call your little liaisons.'

The muscle in his jaw jerked once more. 'You're really trying my patience, you know that?'

Ruby was saved from having to respond when one of the new paralegals poked his head in the door. 'Oops, sorry,' he said, a little red-faced when he recognised Sam. 'I thought the last meeting was supposed to be done by now.'

'It is done,' Ruby assured him, tilting her chin in Sam's direction. When he didn't immediately agree with her she frowned. 'We are done, aren't we, Mr Ventura?'

He studied her with hard eyes that saw far too much for her liking and revealed far too little. 'We're done,' he finally granted. 'For now.'

CHAPTER FIVE

'ALLISON FROM HR has popped up to see you,' Veronica said, poking her head into Ruby's office. 'Have you got a sec?'

'Sure.' Ruby parked her thoughts on the file notes she was making about a new case and ushered Allison into her office. Not that she'd been all that productive. It was five o'clock on Friday night and her concentration had been shot as of about an hour ago. Maybe more. At least *this* Friday night she was going straight home to the safety of her apartment, where there would be wine, her beloved *Law & Order*, and both Ben *and* Jerry waiting for her.

'Hey,' Allison said, taking a seat opposite her. 'So I got your email and I thought I'd come up in person to check if you're serious about this interoffice transfer before I start working on it.'

Ruby tucked a wing of hair behind her ear. After her disastrous meeting with Sam she'd sent Allison an email about transferring out of the Sydney office, but now she wasn't so sure about it. She knew Kent's looked highly on those who expanded their knowledge by working in other offices, but was that really what she wanted to do?

Certainly she'd feel less jumpy if she knew Sam wasn't able to pop his head into her office when she least expected it, or if she didn't have to worry about running into him in the hallway, but wasn't moving to another country a little drastic?

'Ten out of ten would have meant we were in a bed, naked, and we had all night together.'

Okay. Possibly not.

'Yes, I'm serious. I wouldn't mind expanding my horizons and challenging myself a bit more.'

'In another country?'

No, another planet might be better, but apparently Mars was still uninhabitable. 'They say a change is as good as a holiday,' Ruby offered with a shrug. 'And it won't be for ever. I just think I need something a bit different right now.'

Allison gave her a sympathetic smile. 'Man trouble?'

Ruby felt herself flush. 'Sort of.' Hadn't she vowed when she was younger that she'd never let a man interfere with her career as her father had done to her mother?

But that wasn't what was happening here, was it?

'I feel for you,' Allison said. 'And you're in luck. We have a couple of placements coming up. One in the US and the other in London. Do you have a preference or would you like me to put you down for both?'

The US was a little close to where Sam had previously worked. If she moved there and then he returned for work that would defeat the entire purpose of the exercise.

'London,' she said on a decisive note. She'd never been to London. It was cold, yes, but there was the West End, Covent Garden, double-decker buses and, best of all, no distracting boss.

'Okay.' Allison stood up. 'I'll make sure your name goes to the head of the queue. I owe you a favour.'

Ruby knew Allison was referring to the previous year when she'd helped her nephew out of a spot of shoplifting trouble. 'You don't owe me at all,' she said with a mock frown. 'But I appreciate the sentiment.'

'No worries… Oh, hi, Sam.' Allison stepped to the side to allow the man Ruby was dead keen on avoiding into her office. 'Hope you had a nice time interstate yesterday.'

'Very productive, Allison, thank you.'

Of course he already knew Allison's name. She was bright, bubbly and *single*. *And none of your business*, Ruby told herself.

'Great, well, I hope you both enjoy the long weekend.' She waved at Ruby as she left, fanning herself as she passed Sam, a cheeky grin on her face.

Ignoring the butterflies milling around in her stomach at finding herself alone with him, Ruby gave Sam a level look.

'What can I do for you?' she asked, hoping her tone hit somewhere between professional and unaffected.

Sam glanced back at Allison's departing figure. 'You got problems with HR?'

'No.' As Managing Partner, he probably had a right to know her long-term plans at the firm but she had no intention of sharing them at this point. Not when she wasn't completely certain of them herself. 'Allison just stopped by.' Which was true enough.

'Good.' He moved further into her office, closing the door behind him. 'I received your update that we now have fifteen of the original nineteen plaintiffs back on board, as well as five women. That's great news.'

'It is.' Ruby had been ecstatic when the boys had responded so favourably to Sam's pep talk, encouraging their female counterparts to come forward. 'We have a class-action suit again. Thank you. If you hadn't insisted on meeting with them we'd have had more of an uphill battle ahead of us.'

'Don't thank me. We still have an uphill battle ahead of us, but we're a team now. If you need something I'd like to think that you'll call on me to help you get it.'

Ruby nodded, swallowing the weird lump that had formed in her throat. She wondered what it would feel like if they really were a team, with none of this awkward tension between them. 'I appreciate the offer,' she began tentatively. 'But I'm good. Next week we'll file proceedings, and then there will be a mountain of documents to review before—' she stopped as she realised she was rambling. 'You already know the legal procedure.'

'I do,' he agreed wryly. 'And the Star Burger case isn't the only reason I'm here.'

'Sorry.' Feeling as gauche as a first-day trial lawyer, Ruby tried for a smile. 'Why else did you stop by?'

'Lawson Publishing House have their national conference on this weekend and Drew is supposed to attend the keynote address tonight as a thank-you for the work the firm did for them last year. Since Mandy isn't feeling too well right now, he asked me to fill in.' He rubbed the faint stubble on his jaw and Ruby noted the tired lines on the outer edges of his eyes. Maybe he wasn't sleeping any better than she was. 'Since the chairman and I haven't met and you've worked closely with him on one or two issues, Drew thought it would be a good idea for you to attend with me. He apologised for the late notice, but the whole thing shouldn't last for more than an hour. Two at the most.'

In the past Ruby would have had no problem representing the firm at such an event. She'd done so on more than one occasion. But tonight, with Sam? She controlled her breathing as she held his gaze, her mind immediately conjuring up images of him and her, the wall behind her, his body in front. Heat surged low in her pelvis, sparking little tremors of need inside her.

'Apparently we're free to leave after the keynote is finished,' he continued. 'Before that, though, there is a bit of mingling to be done.'

It wasn't the mingling she was worried about. 'I...I...'

Have an appointment with a tub of ice cream? Have to wash my hair? Do my nails?

'You what?' he asked, nonchalantly leaning against the side of her desk and piercing her with a dark look. 'Can't think of anything worse than spending an evening alone with me?'

'I hardly call attending a business function an evening alone with you.'

'I wouldn't either. So why the look of dismay?' His eyes raked over her face. 'Disappointed that it's *not* an evening alone, perhaps?'

The memory of what had happened between them a week ago, of how she had responded to him, lay hot and heavy between them.

'Of course not.' Her chin rose as she fought to slow her heartbeat. 'But what if I already have a date for tonight?'

''Then you'll have to cancel it,' he said so softly she knew it wasn't a suggestion.

She wanted to tell him that if she really did have a date she'd do no such thing, but the look in his eyes stayed her. 'Fine.' She huffed out a breath. 'Fortunately for you, I believe that work is more important than anything else anyway.'

'Work is never more important than anything

else,' he said with such conviction she felt a little taken aback. 'But regardless, this *is* a work function and your commitment to the firm is duly noted.'

'Lucky me.' She closed the law-review tome she'd been consulting earlier with a thud. 'Which hotel is the conference being held at? I can meet you there.'

'No need.' He straightened away from her desk, his eyes cool. 'I've ordered a car.'

Stuck in the back of a car with Sam Ventura during rush-hour traffic...

'Terrific,' she said with a wide smile.

Sam tuned out the keynote speaker's lengthy address and tuned into the blonde sitting beside him. Not hard when his body was already so aware of her it ached.

While he'd been interstate the previous day he'd decided to ignore the searing attraction between the two of them. He'd already witnessed her turning the other way in the corridor when she saw him coming more than once and it annoyed the hell out of him. What did she think he was going to do? Throw her over his shoulder and drag her into the nearest office to ravish her? He'd already told her that he never mixed business with pleasure and it was a code he'd never broken.

Before.

A moody scowl twisted his lips. The truth was, he still wanted her badly and he didn't care about the fact that she worked for him. He didn't care about anything other than taking her and watching her shatter in his arms again until the only name she could form on her well-sated lips was his. It wasn't a desire that made sense, given the strength of it, but it wasn't one he seemed able to fight either.

Much to his consternation.

The whole idea of being led around by his passions was anathema to him. Yes, he went after things he desired, and yes, he was usually successful in achieving them, but he wasn't a risk-taker like Tino, or a win-at-all-costs guy like Dante. He was the easygoing brother. The one least likely to feel deeply about anything or anyone.

Except when it came to Ruby Clarkson.

He took a healthy swallow of the cabernet sauvignon in his glass, easing out a slow breath. The woman was turning out to be a conundrum, and ignoring the stunning attraction between them only seemed to drive his need for her even higher. Would one more night together resolve that? One more night on his terms to work this crazy attraction out of his system. He didn't know, but his body liked that idea a whole lot more than it did avoidance.

He noticed Missy Lawson, the chairman's newly divorced daughter, bearing down on him and glanced at Ruby. She had her hair loose, the shiny golden strands like twin curtains framing her perfect face, her black dress, long enough to be demure in the office, short enough that it showed off her sensational legs. It made a man think about setting his fingers to the zipper at the back and sliding it slowly downward.

'Time for us to leave,' he growled softly, noticing a fine tremor go through her as his hand settled against her lower back. He inhaled through his nose, drawing her rose-tinted scent into his lungs before he thought better of it.

'The keynote's not finished yet,' she whispered back.

'I know.' He glanced over his shoulder to see Missy getting closer. 'I won't tell Drew if you don't.'

Ruby glanced behind him and then tipped her face up to his, her eyes dancing with an impish light that reminded him of the Ruby he had met in that bar two years ago. 'Missy looks like she wants another word with you.'

Sam took Ruby's arm in a light hold. 'Exactly why we have to leave.'

As he was about to surreptitiously tug her towards the exit doors the keynote chose that moment to wrap it up. Polite clapping ensued and before Sam could take control once more he found their way blocked by someone else. A man this time.

'Ruby.' Chester Harris, the stockbroker from Tino and Miller's wedding, zeroed in on Ruby like a heat-seeking missile.

'Sam.' Missy Lawson did the same to him as she barrelled to a halt beside him.

'Chester,' Ruby said with surprise.

'Missy,' Sam said through gritted teeth. 'We were just leaving.'

'My father wants to run a small legal matter past you,' Missy purred. 'It shouldn't take long.'

Sam unclenched his jaw long enough to let Ruby know he'd be no more than five minutes.

'That's fine,' she said, 'I can find my own way home.'

Sam stopped her with a look. 'Do not leave without me this time, Clarkson.' His tone promised all sorts of trouble if she did.

Ruby's eyes flashed like polished emeralds in the bright light of the hotel ballroom, her jaw tight. He didn't know if her curt nod at his blatant order meant that she would wait or not, and he was further irritated when she allowed Chester Harris to take her arm as they walked away. Had he been the date she'd needed to cancel in order to be here with him?

Realising that the knot behind his rib cage was jealousy only made Sam's mood blacker. He really needed to get a handle on Ruby Clarkson and how she made him feel.

Thirty long minutes later he assured John Lawson that his latest author was unlikely to be in breach of any copyright laws, gave Missy what he hoped was a polite smile and went in search of Ruby.

His blood pressure, already raised by Harris's proprietary manner with her earlier, shot a little higher when he found him hemming Ruby in against one of the large supporting pillars in the cavernous room.

'Harris,' he said in a low, dangerous voice. *I believe you have something of mine.* 'I didn't expect to see you here tonight.'

'Sam Ventura.' He gave Sam a smile that displayed every one of his freshly capped teeth. 'The last time we met was at your brother's wedding if I'm not mistaken.'

'Was it?' Sam considered the merits of bruising his knuckles on the other man's jaw and taking a few of those shiny teeth out in the process. If nothing else it would distract him from the unexpectedly possessive thought he'd just had about Ruby being his. It made him feel raw. Exposed.

Ignoring Harris, he stared down at Ruby. 'Ready to go?'

'You're leaving already?' Harris's eyes widened with interest. 'Together?'

'We came together,' Ruby supplied hastily. 'We shared a car.'

They'd shared a lot more than a car and right now Sam didn't give a damn if Harris knew it. 'And now we're leaving. Together,' he finished, setting his hand to the small of Ruby's back as he steered her towards the exit.

Sidestepping his touch, Ruby smiled at various delegates as they worked their way out of the room.

'Why did you have to say that?' she hissed, frowning at him as their limousine driver opened the rear door.

'Get in.' Ignoring her question, Sam ushered her

into the plush interior and followed close behind. Her gaze glittered with feminine outrage as he settled on the leather seat opposite her, which only irritated him more.

'Are you going to answer me?' she demanded hotly.

'No.'

'No?' Ruby all but vibrated against the soft leather seat. 'You just told Sydney's biggest blabbermouth that we were leaving together in a voice that implied we were *leaving together*.'

'How you could ever go out with someone like that I'll never know.'

'I didn't go out with him.'

'Glad to hear it. So why did you take him to Tino and Miller's wedding?'

'None of your business.'

Sam noted her stony profile and stiff shoulders, the colour high along her cheekbones. Could it be that Harris had just been a beard at the wedding? A way of keeping Sam at bay? Irritatingly, if it had been, it had worked.

'Don't worry, I think I know.'

Ruby gave up glaring at the window and glared at him instead. 'Know what?'

'Why you took Harris to the wedding. You wanted me but you didn't want to admit it.'

'You are so full of yourself I'm surprised your enormous ego can fit inside the car with us.'

'And you're snippy.' He leaned forward, his knees

brushing the outside of hers. 'Snippy, prickly and jittery. Now, why is that, do you suppose?'

'I don't know, Sam. You're the one who knows everything, so you tell me.'

'I think you can't forget what happened between us last week any more than I can.' A flush rose up along her cheekbones and he wanted to reach out and tug her onto his lap. 'I think you're not sleeping properly because you can't forget how it felt to have my hands on you.' His voice dropped to a rumbling purr. 'My mouth.'

Her eyelids fluttered shut for a brief second.

'Tell me when you knew it was me,' he pressed softly, not realising how important her answer was until he'd voiced the question.

She frowned across at him, not following where his mind had gone before a cynical smile twisted her lips. 'I don't see what that has to do with anything.'

'Humour me.'

'Why?' she parried. 'If anyone should be asking that question it's me.' She looked down her nose at him. 'After all, you were the one who claimed that a man with any integrity should know if he's ever kissed a woman before.'

It took Sam a moment to place that comment and when he did he laughed. 'You knew it was me that early on, huh? Well, that does stroke my enormous ego. So why the anonymity?'

She shifted restlessly in her seat. 'Maybe I didn't feel like making small talk.'

'And maybe there's more to it than that,' he said, knowing he was right when she narrowed her eyes.

'As I said, I should be the one asking you that question.' She gave him a cool look. 'When *did* you figure out it was me?'

He leaned back against the soft leather upholstery and tried to remember the last time he'd enjoyed talking to a woman as much as he did Ruby. 'I knew the exact moment you turned those frosty green eyes on me,' he said quietly.

She glanced back at him, her eyes suddenly wary. 'If that's true then why didn't *you* say anything at the time?'

'I did. I offered to carry your drinks.'

She bit into her bottom lip, her brows drawn together. 'I thought you were trying to pick me up.'

A grin spread slowly across his face. 'I was.'

'Oh—'

Before she could blast him with yet another fiery put-down a car horn honked and almost immediately their driver swerved, muttering curses as he slammed on the brakes. The car lurched to a sudden halt and Ruby slid from her seat straight into Sam's arms.

Startled, she braced her hands against his shoulders, her breath caught somewhere between her lungs and her throat. He knew because his hands were on either side of her ribcage, right beneath the swell of her soft breasts.

The car started forward, the driver muttering an

apology over his shoulder as he manoeuvred around a stalled taxi in the centre lane.

'What happened?' Ruby asked breathlessly.

'Fate,' he answered roughly, one hand lifting to slide beneath the thick fall of her hair as he brought her mouth to his.

As soon as his lips covered hers she opened for him, her eager tongue tangling with his with a hungry abandon that matched his own.

She moaned softly as he deepened the kiss, her fingernails digging into his shoulders.

'Sam.' His name was a sensual plea on her lips as she met him kiss for kiss, her hands forking into his hair to drag him closer. The pleasure of having her body plastered up against his was exquisite, the taste of her explosive. He wanted to put his mouth all over her, sucking and licking her, particularly between her soft, golden thighs. He told her as much and the sexy little noise she made nearly undid him.

'Yes, angel, kiss me like that.' Ravenous for more, Sam urged her legs to part, pulling her astride his lap, his hands moving lower to slide along her outer thighs, pushing her dress up over the curve of her bottom. A low groan was ripped from his throat as she moved against him in wanton abandon.

'Christ, Ruby.' His lips attacked her neck, his hands fisted in her hair to lock her in place, his blood pumping thickly through his veins. This was exactly how it had been last Friday night. Wild. Uninhibited. *Insatiable.*

'A man could get addicted to this mouth,' he said, taking her bottom lip between his teeth and urging her closer.

She moaned, her lips tracking over his jaw and his chin, her little teeth nipping at his skin.

It felt as if they were both cocooned in a warm, dark room. Just the two of them. Man and woman at their most elemental. No past or future to come between them. No masks and no running.

Just total surrender and a sexual chemistry that blew his mind. His fingers stroked along the edge of her lace panties, his sex-induced brain trying to warn him that he was going too far again. That he needed to stop this madness because—

'Mr Ventura, sir, we have arrived at our destination.'

Because they were in the back of a limousine.

Sam knew Ruby hadn't heard the driver because her fingers were still fumbling with the buttons on his shirt. For a second he nearly closed the partition between them and the driver and let her continue. Then sanity asserted itself. 'Ruby, sweetheart.' He took her hands in his. 'We have to stop.'

'Stop?'

She blinked up at him, her slumberous gaze turning from glazed to glaring in a heartbeat.

'Oh, God.' She pushed off his lap and fell awkwardly onto the opposite seat, smoothing her skirt down her legs, regret written all over her beautiful face. 'Of course we have to stop.'

'Like we should have stopped last Friday night?'

'Absolutely.'

'And I suppose you want to forget about this *incident* just like you've *forgotten* the last one.'

'Absolutely.'

For some reason her ready agreement only fuelled his irritation. So did that regal, untouchable air she cloaked herself in. Something that might have been a little more effective if her lips weren't still swollen and moist from his kisses. 'Only you haven't forgotten last Friday night any more than I have. Isn't that the truth, Ruby?'

'The truth is we work together, and Chester is probably spreading salacious stories about us right now.'

'In this case he'd be right.'

He knew it wasn't fair to goad her like that but, dammit, she was making him feel as if he was fully responsible for that kiss and she'd been as into it as he had been.

'He would not be right,' she snapped, scowling at him.

'He would. But it's late. If you want to argue some more about it you'll have to invite me up for coffee.'

Clearly embarrassed to find that they were parked outside her apartment building, Ruby threw open the car door, nearly catching their circumspect chauffeur in the chest. 'That,' she said loftily, 'will never happen again. I learn from my mistakes. I don't repeat them.'

'Pity.' Sam's eyes narrowed, his fingers mana-cling her wrist before she could toss her hair over her shoulder and exit the car. 'Because this time I would have said yes. But fair warning, sweetheart—the next time my mouth is on yours we'll be horizontal and I'll be taking my time. That is,' he paused, his thumb stroking lightly over the pulse pounding in her wrist 'after you've asked me nicely.'

Ruby pulled her wrist out from under his hold and shot him a fulminating glare. 'You cannot possibly imagine how much I dislike you right now.'

Sam couldn't help himself: he laughed. 'Oh, I think I can.'

He watched the long, lean lines of her body as she stalked straight-backed away from the car. When she was safely inside her glass security door he leaned his head back against the seat, gave the driver his address and asked himself what it was about this woman that drove every civilised thought from his head. Even now, when he told himself to go and find a nice, even-tempered woman who knew how to ap-preciate him, he wanted this one with a fierceness that defied logic.

Ruby Clarkson, it turned out, was more than a simple conundrum; she was a colossal pain in his rear end.

CHAPTER SIX

RUBY WOKE THE following morning with a start, sitting bolt upright in her bed, a particularly carnal dream of her and Sam naked and sweaty and *horizontal* front and centre in her mind.

Groaning, she collapsed back against her fluffy pillows and stared at the ceiling. If last night had proved anything at all it was that her willpower to keep away from the man who haunted her days and her nights was practically zero once he put his hands on her, making that potential job in London look better and better.

Determined that next Friday night she was going to keep well away from him, she rolled over and checked the time.

Molly had stayed at a friend's the night before so she wouldn't be bursting in any second to push her to do yoga.

Maybe she'd skip it today. She had a ton of work to do anyway, along with another embarrassing escapade with her boss to try to forget about.

God, when would she learn?

Not any time soon, it seemed. Thankful it was Saturday, the first day of the long weekend and she'd have no reason to see Sam for three whole days, she flipped onto her stomach and thought about going back to sleep. Then her phone pinged, sending her senses onto high alert.

Miller's name flashed on the screen and Ruby groaned out loud. Oh, no! Long weekend. Beach house. A month ago Miller had suggested that they have a girly weekend together. How had she forgotten that?

'Would you believe I'm nearly ready?' Ruby hedged, answering the phone as she stumbled out of bed and staggered into the bathroom.

'How could you forget?' Miller complained. 'I left a reminder message on your phone last night.'

She had? 'Sorry, I didn't get it. I'm a really bad friend.'

'Were you working late again? Is that the problem?'

'Yeah… I had a function and…never mind.' She peered at her wan reflection in the mirror, pressing on the dark circles beneath her eyes. 'Am I too late to still make it?'

'Of course not. But there's been a slight change of plan. Red is a bit under the weather, so he and Tino are joining us. I hope that's okay.'

Red was Redmond Ventura, Miller and Tino's adorable toddler and, as the first baby in their circle of friends, a pseudo-nephew to both her and Molly.

'Of course it's okay,' Ruby said. 'I'll even take Red tomorrow morning so you and Valentino can have a sleep in together.'

'I knew I loved you.' Miller laughed. 'By the way, Tino has— Oh, drat, Red's crying.'

'Go and get him,' Ruby urged, grabbing her tooth-brush and turning the shower on. 'I'll be there in… twenty minutes?'

Miller snorted. 'Sure. See you in an hour, then.'

Ringing off, Ruby ducked into the shower. She had a special bottle of champagne in the fridge to help celebrate the long weekend with her best friend. The fact that she'd forgotten that as well was a testament to how much Sam Ventura was messing with her head.

But not any more. As of now, Ruby would banish the man from her mind and her life and pull herself together. And a weekend away with Miller and her family was just the ticket. She wouldn't have time to moon over Sam, or wonder what he was doing and with whom he was doing it. She certainly wouldn't have time to think about kissing him.

Fair warning, sweetheart, the next time my mouth is on yours we'll be horizontal and I'll be taking my time.

Good grief! She blew out an unsteady breath, a rush of desire turning her insides hot and shivery at just the memory of how he had kissed her in the back of their limousine.

Just behind the driver.

She groaned, shaking her head. A week ago her life had been ticking along perfectly. She had work, yoga, good friends and Netflix. Now she had angst, indecision, erotic dreams and *longing*.

The longing was the worst. It was like a secret weakness she didn't want to admit to having. Instinctively she knew that if she ever slept with Sam again she'd be changing her life for him before she knew it, followed by crying with her friends when it all went wrong. Because it would go wrong. It was inevitable. Sam was a heartbreaker. And he was too demanding, too arrogant. He would want more from her than she was prepared to give and she was very afraid she'd give it anyway.

A sense of foreboding flashed across her skin like a cold draught. Her father walking out on them all those years ago had left her with a natural sense of caution when it came to men that had always held her in good stead. So no, she was not going to let Sam any closer than he already had been *ever again*. That would be like carrying a metal pole onto a football field in the middle of an electric storm and hoping not to get struck by lightning.

'Good pep talk.' She smiled at her reflection and skipped out of the bathroom. Miller's beach house beckoned, where she could swim, chat, play with Red and relax to her heart's content.

Quickly pulling on white shorts and a striped top, she pushed her feet into her favourite beaten-up espadrilles, packed her bag and raced down the stairs, thankful that she only had to wait a few minutes before her cab driver arrived.

'Double Bay Wharf,' she said, settling back against the seat and closing her eyes. Too late she remembered that her e-reader, with the newly downloaded crime novel on it, was on her bedside table. She hoped Miller had some trashy novel she could lose herself in just in case the champagne didn't do the job of getting Sam out of her head at night.

Arriving at the wharf, she skipped down the wooden gangplank towards Valentino's latest motorised toy, *Miller's Way,* and felt lighthearted as she smiled at a one-legged seagull that was completely unconcerned about her presence.

Rows of pristine white yachts bobbed side by side in the bright sunshine, and the deep blue of the harbour sparkled as if tiny diamonds had been dropped from the sky and floated across the surface as mystical as rainbows. It was a good day to be alive and she had three whole days of bliss stretched out in front of her. Three whole days of rest and relaxation and not wondering about whether she was going to accidentally run into a certain somebody when she least expected it.

Sam brooded as Valentino bent over the boat engine, absently stroking the black and tan puppy in his arms.

'Wrench,' Valentino said, his head stuck inside the engine bay.

Sam handed him the tool. The restless fluff-ball wriggled in his arms, eager to explore his new surroundings. He'd had the thing for two hours. A rash decision that was as unlike him as his actions with Ruby since returning to Sydney. And he couldn't exactly blame jet lag for his loss of control last night, or for picking up the puppy at the rescue centre. Perhaps he had some superbug eating away at his brain bit by bit.

'I said wrench.' Valentino frowned at him. 'This is a ratchet.'

Sam glanced into the toolbox. He pulled out the wrench.

'You sure you're okay?' Tino glanced up at him.

'Fine.'

Tino grunted. 'About as fine as this engine.'

Ignoring his brother's pointed comment, he focused on the engine trouble. 'Will you get it running?'

Valentino threw him a look as if to say *Will the sun set in the west?* He stuck his head back in the hull. 'I'd better. Miller's been looking forward to this weekend all month. And Ruby's bringing champagne. Hopefully on ice.'

Sam's whole body went rigid at Tino's throwaway comment. The puppy whimpered and he eased his grip from around its soft belly. 'Ruby?' Part of the reason he had made the early-morning decision to take his brother up on his offer to spend the long weekend at the beach house was to put some space between Ruby and his sudden obsession to dial her number every five seconds. Why hadn't he asked Tino if she would be coming along?

Because he hadn't wanted Tino to question his sudden interest in Ruby's whereabouts until he had some plausible answers that made sense. And look how spectacularly that had backfired on him now. He frowned at the puppy that stared back at him with huge, guileless brown eyes. He didn't know what had possessed him to get the mutt either. He'd been walking past the animal rescue centre and the next thing he knew he was signing papers and being instructed on brands of puppy food.

'You know, I have a mind to call back that fancy-arsed mechanic...' Tino muttered, issuing a string of curse words under his breath. 'Guy wouldn't know a carburettor from a custard tart.'

Sam ignored his brother's mumblings. He was still reeling from the fact that Ruby would soon be joining them.

Ruby for a whole three days with his brother and fiercely protective sister-in-law in tow...

'God, I'm good!' Tino smirked as the boat's engine rumbled to life beneath his feet, wiping his hands on an old rag.

'So about the weekend...' Sam began, thinking that he didn't care if Tino thought his behaviour was strange or not.

'Yeah?' Tino looked at him curiously. 'What about it?'

The puppy squirmed like a bag of worms in his

arms, yapping at something over his shoulder. Sam turned in time to see Ruby coming aboard and his heart did a weird flip inside his chest. She looked confident and radiant, her long hair pulled into a haphazard ponytail, a dazzling smile curving her soft pink lips. He'd rarely seen her without make-up and right now she looked golden and youthful and more beautiful than ever, like a sun goddess come down to earth to shine just for him.

Catching the uncharacteristically poetic sentiment, he shook his head. It didn't seem to matter to his brain that she was completely off-limits to him. She excited him as no other woman ever had and, while he might not like that on an elemental level, if he was completely honest with himself he didn't want it to stop either.

Ruby didn't notice Sam until she had both feet planted on the boat. If she had when she'd only had one foot on board she might have turned and run. As it was she could only stop and stare at him.

He wore aviator sunglasses, his long, lean body encased in a T-shirt that emphasised his flat belly and wide shoulders, and fitted board shorts that hugged his muscular thighs. His feet were jammed into boat shoes, his arms full of an exuberant black and brown puppy with one adorable ear folded forward. Both their gazes were trained on her. It struck her almost immediately that she had never seen Sam in casual wear before and he was ten times more dangerous to her this way than in a custom-made suit. Heat seared her insides, her body uncaring that last night he had been so arrogant she'd wanted to throttle him.

As she watched Sam lowered the squirming bundle of fluff onto the deck and it raced towards her. She instinctively went down on her haunches and the puppy jumped into her arms, licking her face.

'Some guard dog he is,' Sam grumbled, coming to a stop in front of her.

Finding it hard to hold herself aloof with the puppy all over her, Ruby laughed joyously. 'He knows I'm a friend. Don't you, boy? Girl?'

'Boy,' Sam replied, just as Miller came up from below deck carrying Redmond in her arms.

'Hey, Ruby.' Miller hugged her as she stood up. 'Forty-five minutes. I'm impressed. By the way, Tino invited Sam, so our girls' weekend has definitely been gatecrashed.'

'So I see,' Ruby murmured.

'Let me take your bag.'

'I've got it.' Sam reached for it first and hoisted it onto his shoulder before Ruby could object.

'Thanks, Sam.' Miller grinned widely, shifting Red to her other arm so that he could reach out and play with Ruby's hair. 'I'm so glad you're here. Tino, Ruby's—'

'Here, I know.' Valentino pushed out of the engine bay one-handed and came up behind his wife, taking an excited Redmond from her arms. 'Glad you could make it, Ruby. And right on time.'

The puppy jumped up at her again, his nails scoring the skin on her knee. Ruby winced and grabbed his paws, petting his head. 'You're going to be a giant, aren't you?'

'Sorry.' Sam moved forward. 'He hasn't learnt any manners yet.'

'He's yours?' She was surprised. She hadn't expected Sam to be a pet person. Pets seemed so permanent for a man who wasn't the relationship type.

He picked up the puppy and wiped slobber off his face as it licked him. 'Yes, he's mine,' Sam answered her. 'I just got him this morning from the rescue centre.'

'Someone disowned him?'

'They did more than that.' His voice deepened with disgust. 'He was thrown into a wheelie bin with his brothers and sisters.'

'Oh, you poor thing.' Instinctively Ruby reached out her hand to stroke between his ears, the move bringing her closer to Sam than she would have liked. 'What's his name?'

'Mutt.'

'Mutt?' She scowled at him. 'You can't call him that.'

'I haven't named him yet. Maybe Shep.'

'Too passé,' she said. 'What about Caesar?'

'And give him unnecessary illusions of grandeur? There's only room for one alpha in this pack.'

Ruby rolled her eyes, unable to prevent a smile from forming on her lips. 'I hope he gives you a run for your money.'

Miller laughed. 'He's already got Sam wrapped around his over-large paw, from what I can see.'

'Looks can be deceiving, Millsy,' Sam countered. 'What would you call him?' he asked Ruby.

Ruby studied the puppy, tapping a finger against her bottom lip. 'Kong.'

'Kong?'

The scepticism in his voice made her laugh. 'He's going to be enormous,' she said; 'you can tell by the ears and the feet.'

Sam turned the dog to face him, holding him at arm's length. 'Are you a Kong?'

The puppy barked enthusiastically and Miller laughed. 'He likes it.'

'And it's a hell of a lot better than Mutt,' Tino drawled. 'Come on, Red,' he said, 'time to get underway.'

'Ah, wait…' Ruby trailed off as three pairs of eyes turned towards her. Unbidden, her gaze sought Sam's. She wanted to say that she had changed her mind about the weekend. That something had come up. Something urgent and completely unavoidable. Only her fuzzy brain couldn't produce a single excuse that sounded urgent or unavoidable. Especially with Sam looking at her with that half-cocked grin as if he knew exactly what she was thinking.

Her pregnant pause lengthened into uncomfortable territory, the sun beating down hot and inviting on her head, the waves gently lapping at the side of the hull.

'Did you forget something?' Miller asked. 'We probably have it at the house if you have.'

Ruby had that same embarrassing feeling she'd had two years ago. The one where she made a mountain out of a molehill, thinking that Sam had felt more for her than he really had. The one that had made her sit by the phone all weekend, not even questioning if he'd call, but actually believing that he would.

'No,' she said, forcing a smile to her lips. 'I didn't forget a thing.'

If Sam wasn't bothered by having her around this weekend then she wasn't going to be bothered having him around either. Or at least she wouldn't *show* that she was bothered.

After docking at Tino and Miller's private jetty, Ruby made a beeline for the state-of-the-art kitchen, fetching two mugs from the kitchen cupboard and reaching for the old-fashioned kettle on the stovetop. 'Tea?'

'Tea?' Miller crinkled her nose in disgust, placing a box of fresh produce on the granite countertop. 'Is it too early for champagne?'

'Where do you want these?' Sam stepped inside with another box of supplies under one arm.

'Over there,' Miller said, indicating an empty place on the bench behind Ruby.

Quickly skirting sideways, Ruby sucked in her breath as Sam's elbow brushed her stomach on his way past.

'Sorry.'

'No, I should have…' Ruby pressed closer against the sink and ducked around him to move to the other side of the bench, ignoring his delicious scent as it wafted into her nose.

'Great house,' Sam said easily, and Ruby envied him his composure. Her pulse was beating dangerously fast yet again. 'I can see why you bought it.'

'I know. We loved it as soon as we saw it.' Miller smiled, looking between her and Sam. 'You know, the place two houses along is up for sale.'

'That so?' Sam said.

'Yep.' Miller rinsed Redmond's sipper cup under the tap and stowed it on a shelf. 'Maybe you should look at buying it. Then, when you find a woman to settle down with, our kids can spend summers together, running back and forth between each other's houses.'

'You got it all planned out, Millsy,' Sam said with an easy smile.

'It's the organiser in her,' Ruby interjected. For some reason Miller's words had conjured up a picture so sweet it made Ruby's chest ache. 'But Sam isn't interested in relationships. Isn't that right, Sam?'

Sam took a bottle of water from the fridge, unscrewed the cap and raised it to his lips, his eyes seeing more than she wanted him to see. 'Depends how good the house is.'

Miller laughed.

Ruby didn't.

'And the type of relationship we're talking about,' he added softly.

Ruby's heartbeat picked up at the way he was looking at her, the lid of the kettle she'd been unknowingly fiddling with clattering to the counter as it slipped out of her grasp. Snatching it up, she jammed it back into place. 'The permanent type, of course.'

He shifted closer to her, subtly hemming her in against the hob. 'Perhaps I just haven't met the right woman yet.'

'Really?' She gave him a withering look. 'You're going to play that hand?'

'What's wrong, angel? You looking for love and happily-ever-after?'

'No.'

She absolutely was not looking for that.

'Ah, well, there goes my plan to ask you to marry me and put me out of my misery.'

Knowing that she only had herself to blame for this conversation, Ruby told herself not to bite. She did anyway. 'Marry you?' She nearly choked on the word. 'I wouldn't marry you if you were the last man on earth and civilisation relied on us to…to…' She felt her face flush with heat.

'Procreate?'

She heard the laughter in his voice and her lips clamped together. 'Exactly!'

'Oh, well. You can't blame a man for trying. A word of advice, though…' He nodded over her shoulder at the kettle. 'You might want to put some water in that before you boil it. It works better that way.'

Exasperated at how easily he riled her, Ruby glared at his broad back, refusing to admire the width of his shoulders or the narrowness of his hips as he strolled out of the back door.

'You going to explain all that or do I have to work for it?' Miller said into the ensuing silence.

Ruby glanced over at her, appalled to realise that she'd forgotten her friend was even in the room with them. 'What's to explain?' she hedged. 'He likes to provoke me and, fool that I am, I fall for it every time.'

'I was talking more about the wicked sexual tension between the two of you,' Miller said, fanning her face. 'It was a little hot in here for a while.'

Ruby let out a sigh. 'You're not going to let up on this, are you?'

'Of course I will.' Miller gave her a too-innocent look. 'If you don't want to tell me what's going on between the two of you then I completely respect that.'

'Fine. We slept together—or, rather, we had sex.' She winced as Miller's jaw hit the floor. 'Yes, you heard me right. And it was against a wall. At the Herzog party.'

There it was, out in the open. No big deal. She was only glad Miller wouldn't realise it had been her first time. If she knew that then it would totally be a big deal. She'd want to know, why Sam? Why then? And how did Ruby answer that without telling her best friend that no other man had ever affected her as Sam did?

'The Herzog party? As in *the* Herzog party? The one anybody who is anybody tries to get an invitation to every year?'

'Is there any other?'

'Well, then.' Miller set her shoulders as if she were about to mine iron ore from a deep quarry. 'We're going to need something stronger than tea. Or champagne.'

Ruby groaned into her hands. 'Please don't make it out to be more than it is. It's never happening again.'

Miller placed a crystal tumbler on the bench in front of her. 'Uh-huh…'

'It's not! I swear.'

'You know I want details.' Miller poured a measure of Johnny Walker into both their glasses. 'How? Why? Which wall?' She grinned as Ruby made a face. 'How good was it? That kind of thing. I mean, the Ventura boys have a bit of a reputation, so I'd be surprised if it wasn't good, but…'

'It wasn't good.' Ruby sipped the amber liquid and let the warmth of it settle in the pit of her stomach. 'It was fantastic. But it was a one-off thing.'

'Uh-huh.'

'Would you stop saying that?' she griped. 'It was.'

'Why?' Miller sat down on a bar stool and eyed her speculatively.

'Because, well…why would it happen again?'

'Because he looks at you like you're a tinderbox

he wants to set a match to and you're so on edge you look like you need that match.'

'Miller, be serious!' Ruby implored. 'I'm not into sex for the sake of it, you know that. And he's my boss. There's only one way that can end. And it's not well.'

'Hmm, his being your boss is a bit of an issue, but it's not the end of the world. Lots of bosses and employees get married.'

'Are you listening to yourself?' Ruby asked, her brows nearly hitting her hairline at the hopeful tone in Miller's voice. 'You've gone from sex against a wall to a white dress and church bells in a matter of seconds. Being married has clearly fried your brain.'

'Can you imagine how much fun it would be if you married Sam, though?' Miller's blue eyes lit up with glee. 'We could—'

'Do nothing!' Ruby used her courtroom voice to cut off her friend's romantic diatribe before it got started. The last thing she needed was her loved-up friend playing matchmaker or, heaven forbid, putting unwanted ideas into her own head.

'Okay, maybe that was a step too far, but I am grappling with the concept that you, Ms Proper Lady Lawyer Extraordinaire, had hot, crazy sex at a party!'

'I know. But can we not talk about it any more? I'm trying to forget it even happened.'

'Not that you have, have you?' Miller asked softly.

'Can I plead the Fifth on that?'

'No.' Miller laughed. 'Australia doesn't have amendments. And I'm not trying to embarrass you. I just want you to relax a little, Rubes, be happy. You deserve it. Not all men are bad, you know. Sam's not.'

'So says the woman who got the last good one.'

'The last good what?'

'Apple,' Ruby filled in quickly as Valentino strolled into the room and slipped his arm around his wife's waist.

Picking up on her cue not to mention any of this to her husband, Miller gave him a searing kiss to distract him. It worked and Ruby slipped out of the back door unnoticed.

Feeling slightly niggled, she kicked off her espadrilles and stepped onto sun-warmed paving stones, sighing at the blissful invitation of the blue-tiled infinity pool that looked as if it continued into the even bluer waters of Elvina Bay.

Crouching down on her haunches, she trailed her fingers across the surface of the pool, enjoying the cool deliciousness of the water as it trickled between her fingers.

Redmond's delightful baby laugh caught her attention and she glanced up to see Sam lying on the lawn, pretending to struggle beneath the combined weight of the toddler and the puppy.

'Okay, okay, you got me.' He groaned, taking care to keep the puppy from launching himself on Redmond and knocking the baby over. 'Ouch, Kong, that's my finger.' He ruffled the dog's fur and gave him a playful push. The puppy loved it, launching himself even harder at his new master.

A strange sensation rushed into Ruby's chest as she watched them play. So he was good with kids and animals. And he was smart. Attractive. Of course he was. All the Ventura men were. It was some freak gene that made them tall, god-like and irresistible to unsuspecting women.

You want to get married and put me out of my misery?

God, he was an ass!

A *too tempting* ass as he leaned up on one hand, his powerful biceps bunching as he moved, his wide chest the perfect foil for the toddler snuggled up against him. He bent his dark head to Redmond's, nuzzling his fine baby hair and making him giggle with helpless delight.

That was just unfair, she thought, forcing her gaze back to the pool. He was unfair. Why did he have to come back to Sydney and turn her life upside down? Why did he have to kiss her? Touch her? Make love to her?

Miller's gentle prodding that she wanted Ruby to be happy played back inside her head. She *was* happy. *Very* happy. Or she had been until Sam had blown back into her life! And, while Miller saw Sam as one of the 'good' ones, that was only because she was married to his brother. She was blinkered. Ruby had already experienced Sam walking away from her once without a backward glance. She didn't want that to happen again. Something inside her warned her that she wouldn't cope as well as she had the first time.

Suddenly realising that Sam was watching her, she let out a slow breath and attempted to marshal her chaotic emotions. Seeing her still crouched by the pool, the puppy cocked his head, his floppy ear bouncing as he scampered towards her.

'Watch the pool,' she cautioned as he bounded along the edge on unstable baby legs. He lapped at her face and she wiped her cheek with the back of her hand. 'You have to stop doing that,' she laughed.

Having followed, Sam offered her a hand up, his other wrapped around Redmond's chubby legs, balancing the toddler high on his hip like a natural.

Ignoring his hand as politely as possible, Ruby stumbled to her feet. 'I didn't know you were going to be here this weekend,' she said on a breathless note, somehow needing him to know that she hadn't planned this. That she wasn't *chasing* him.

'And wished that I wasn't,' he concluded. 'Am I right?'

Ruby shot him a quick glance, unsure how to respond to that in a way that wouldn't ratchet the tension between them even higher.

'Jesus, Ruby,' he growled under his breath. 'I'm not going to jump you. Not without an invitation anyway.'

'All evidence to the contrary,' she retorted, miffed at his arrogance and the fact that if he was to touch her right now she'd probably dissolve into a puddle of lustful cravings. She hadn't slept properly since he'd crashed back into her life, and her defences were clearly suffering as a result.

'That's a low blow.' His bedroom brown eyes locked with hers. 'You wanted that kiss in the cab last night as much as I did.'

'I'm not going to argue with you, Sam. It's pointless.'

'So is pretending that we don't want each other,' he said softly.

'No, it's not,' she denied. 'It makes everything a lot less complicated.'

He threw her a shrewd look. 'Less complicated or more?'

'Less,' she said vigorously. 'Definitely less.'

'I don't know, angel. It's not less complicated for me. In fact, it's downright difficult.'

Sam's hooded gaze travelled down over her throat and breasts that felt heavy and achy, and farther to her bare legs and feet before slowly making its way back to her eyes, heating her up in the process and leaving her in no doubt as to exactly how he found it difficult.

'That's just sex, Sam,' she said, glad Red was too young to understand a word they were saying. 'You can get that from anyone.'

'You're wrong, it wasn't just sex.' He let the squirming toddler down beside a beach ball he was trying to reach. 'It was incredible and I want it again.' His voice grew rough. 'I want *you* again.'

Ruby's heart thundered inside her chest, her whole

body leaning towards his even though she hadn't moved. 'What happened to your credo of not mixing business with pleasure?' she asked huskily.

A sparkle entered his eyes. 'For you I'm willing to make an exception.'

Red made a sound of frustration and Sam bent to scoop the toddler into his arms once more before sauntering back towards the house, the puppy on his heels.

'I'm not, Sam,' she called after him with belligerent finality.

Sam turned back slowly, a wry smile curving his lips. 'And that's your choice.'

Ruby gnashed her teeth together at his easy capitulation. If it was her choice, why did it feel more like a battle? A battle she was waging with herself?

Frustrated, she stared out at the tranquil view but quite unable to take it in. If it was her choice, how was it that every day she saw him, every minute she spent with him, she wanted him more? And what would happen if she did the unthinkable and gave in to the chemistry between them again? Who would be there to catch her if she fell?

CHAPTER SEVEN

THE FOLLOWING MORNING when Ruby stepped into the kitchen she felt bright and eager to start the day.

Sam was wrong. It was a *lot* less complicated to ignore the attraction between them, not more so. She'd done it all night at dinner the night before and she'd had a great time.

She'd been civil to Sam, talking with him and laughing at his jokes, listening to him and Tino recount stories of their childhood and not even noticing the way his black shirt had turned his eyes the same colour and hugged his muscular chest to perfection. Nor had she trembled when he'd accidently brushed up against her while they'd done the cleaning up together, and her heart definitely hadn't beat faster when she'd bid everyone goodnight and felt Sam's dark gaze trained on her the length of the hallway that led to the bedrooms, staring at the ceiling for an hour afterwards until she'd heard his heavy tread take him to his own room.

And if she could truly convince herself of all that she'd consider dropping law to follow Molly into the theatre.

The problem was that she had no idea how to switch off her emotions around Sam. Nothing in her past experiences had equipped her to deal with how she felt when she was in his arms, and it was nothing short of terrifying.

Not expecting to find anyone up, she came to an abrupt halt in the doorway when she noticed Sam sprawled out asleep on the wide modular sofa.

She must have disturbed him because he stirred, groaning as he rolled onto his side, blinking inky black lashes as he looked across at her. Yawning, he rubbed his belly, his T-shirt riding up in the process, making her breath hitch.

As if he caught the sound, his gaze gave her a thorough sweep, making her aware that she was wearing nothing but a silky nightshirt over cotton panties.

Should have dressed first, idiot, she berated herself.

'You can come in, Ruby,' he rumbled sleepily. 'I won't bite.'

Unfortunately Ruby remembered that he did. Right on that sensitive spot where her neck joined her shoulder. 'I thought maybe Redmond would be up. I was going to take him so Miller and Valentino could sleep in together.'

'They're not here.'

About to head back to her room to put more clothes on, Ruby stopped and swung around to find Sam sitting up, his long legs wide apart, his broad shoulders hunched slightly forward as he stroked Kong's ears. 'What do you mean, they're not here?'

'Miller received a phone call early this morning saying that her mother is in hospital. Since Red was already up, they decided to head back to be with her.'

'In hospital? Is she okay?'

'She fell on her way to the bathroom. Suspected broken wrist and ankle.'

'Oh, that's terrible.' Ruby stared, stunned. 'I should call her. Check how she is.' Halfway across the room to retrieve her phone, she stopped. 'Wait. They took the yacht?'

'They did.'

'So how are we going to get back?'

'I told Tino I'd take care of it.'

Ruby's eyes narrowed. 'You'd take care of it. What does that mean?'

Sam passed a hand through his hair, stifling another yawn. 'It means I'll take care of it. I didn't want to worry Miller with the logistics. She was frazzled enough.'

Ruby rubbed her forehead. He might not have wanted to worry Miller, but she really didn't like the idea that she was now stranded at the beach house with Sam. Alone. 'What time was this? Why didn't anyone wake me?'

'It was about five-thirty. No one wanted to wake you.'

'They woke you,' Ruby countered. 'Why not me?'

Sam glanced at the ball of fur at his feet and scowled. 'Tino and Miller didn't wake me. He did. Apparently mutts don't keep normal sleeping hours.'

Any other time his disgruntled scowl might have been endearing, but Ruby wasn't in an affable mood. 'So we're stranded here?'

'I hardly think you can call us stranded. I can phone any time and charter a boat to come and pick us up.'

'So why haven't you done it already?'

Sam gave her a narrow-eyed look, clearly not liking her tone. 'I don't know, Ruby,' he drawled dangerously. 'Maybe because it's only seven in the morning and even charter companies have operating hours. And I fell back asleep. Is that a good enough reason for you?'

Ignoring his rhetorical question, she scowled as he pushed to his feet and ambled into the kitchen. Ruby unconsciously tracked his movements, mortifyingly aware of everything about him from his broad shoulders all the way down to his muscular thighs and well-shaped feet. A curl of heat smouldered deep inside her.

'Want a coffee?'

Aware that she'd been caught staring, she blinked, irritation at her own lack of self-control overriding her embarrassment. The man knew how good-looking he was. It wasn't as if he wasn't used to women staring at him.

'No.' She raised her chin. 'What I want is to go home.'

Ignoring her statement, Sam started fiddling with the dials on the coffee machine.

'Did you hear me?' she asked briskly. Now that

Miller and Valentino weren't here to act as buffers she saw no reason to continue to hang around and pretend that she and Sam were going to be able to get along.

'I think the charter company in Circular Quay heard you,' he said, not bothering to turn around.

'Good.' Ruby tapped her foot to keep a lid on her escalating emotions. 'I hope they send someone over quickly.' She crossed her arms over her chest, glaring at his broad back. 'Did you plan this?'

Sam turned slowly towards her, his expression inscrutable. 'Did I plan what?' His tone was low and silky and clearly annoyed. 'Miller's mother's accident?' He placed the flats of his palms down on the granite bench between them, a dangerous glint darkening his eyes. 'Yeah. I took my private jet over to her house early this morning, knocked her down in her hallway and made it back in time to let Kong out for a toilet break. Not bad, eh?'

Ruby pressed her lips together at his sarcastic tone, determined to keep a lid on her temper. 'That wasn't what I meant and you know it. I was talking about Miller and Valentino leaving. If someone had woken me I could have gone with them.'

'My apologies,' Sam said in a voice cold enough to freeze liquid nitrogen. 'It wasn't that you thought I'd injured an old lady in my quest to have you, just that you think I'm so desperate to get you into my bed that I'd orchestrate Miller and Tino leaving without you. Is that it?'

Okay, put like that, it did seem a tad…*hysterical*. Not that she'd admit as much to him.

'Such a high opinion of me, Miss Clarkson,' he continued with ruthless precision. 'What will you accuse me of next? Kidnapping? Unlawful imprisonment? A man could get at least twenty years for any one of those crimes with the right lawyer.'

'Don't be ridiculous,' she snapped, rubbing her brow.

'I'm not the one being ridiculous, angel. You are.'

She knew that. She was just too strung-out to care. 'And stop calling me angel.' When he did it reminded her of how it had felt to be pressed up against his hard, hot body. And how it would feel to be there again.

'You know, I'm not sure if I should live down to your clearly heinous opinion of me and drag you into the bedroom to have my way with you, or walk out of here and let you find your own way home.' He glared at her so hard Ruby felt like a bug under a microscope. 'Now, do you want a damned coffee or not?'

'Yes, I want a damned coffee.' She needed something to get through the debacle of being stranded in this beautiful house, in this beautiful beach setting, with a man who drove her crazy.

'And just so we're clear,' Sam said with deadly emphasis, 'I don't need to resort to underhand tactics to seduce a woman.' He slapped a mug down on the bench in front of her but didn't let go when she reached for the handle.

'I'm very upfront and honest about my needs.'

'And I'm not?'

'Not even close.'

Ruby gripped the handle of the mug, unconsciously registering the warmth of where he had held it. 'Well, at least you can't accuse me of breaking a promise,' she said, turning her back on him.

'Excuse me?'

'Forget it.' She wished she hadn't said anything because she could hear that she'd piqued his interest.

'That was a pointed comment. Explain it.'

'No.'

She put the mug to her lips, her eyes going wide when he rounded the bench to stand in front of her.

Run, an inner voice whispered, *fast*.

'Let me put it another way,' he warned softly. 'You're not leaving this kitchen until you explain yourself.'

'Really?' She lifted her chin belligerently. 'And what if I don't?'

'Then you might well be able to charge me with kidnapping *and* unlawful imprisonment.'

Ruby thought about her options, deciding by the determined jut of his jaw that they were most likely limited. 'Fine.' She huffed out a breath. 'You want to know what I meant, I'll tell you.' She took a quick, fortifying sip of coffee, which was irritatingly delicious. 'Two years ago you walked me home, kissed me breathless and then made some banal promise to call me and never did. Not only that, but the next day I also find out that you escorted another woman to the polo.' Her lips pursed in a moue of distaste. 'I always wondered if you told her that you'd been locking lips with me the night before or if you just moved on without a thought?'

Sam frowned. 'I didn't take anyone to the polo. I went alone.'

'You either think I'm completely daft, Sam, or you have an appalling memory.' She rolled her eyes at his deepening frown. 'Skinny? Beautiful? Redhead? Ring any bells?'

'Ruth Simons?' He stared at her. 'She wasn't my date. She approached me to say hello, we talked about old times and then we went our separate ways. And no, I didn't mention that I spent the night before kissing you *breathless* because it would have been none of her damned business.'

Was he telling the truth?

A litany of her father's broken promises spiralled through her head:

'See you at your softball game this weekend, Rubelicious!'

'Let's go out for your birthday this year, somewhere special for once...'

'I'll call you tomorrow, pumpkin. I promise.'

And her mother's time-honoured advice: *'If you let men walk all over you, Ruby Jane, they'll treat you like a doormat for ever.'*

'It doesn't matter,' Ruby said, confusion and uncertainty replacing the flush of anger that had driven her emotions higher. 'None of it matters.'

Refusing to let her retreat, Sam stepped into her personal space, looming over her. 'I think it does.' His astute gaze held hers. 'I was wrong to say that I'd call you and then not follow through. I hurt you, I think. I'm sorry.'

Shocked by the sincerity of his apology, all Ruby could do was stare up at him.

'It's okay,' Ruby whispered, hating the thready quality in her voice that clearly depicted the hurt she hadn't wanted him to see. 'It's not as if it has any bearing on the here and now.'

'It clearly does or you wouldn't have mentioned it.' His hands came up to curve around her shoulders. 'And you need to know that I *was* intending to call you. I just…' He grimaced. 'I got cold feet at the last minute. I can't explain it other than to say that I wasn't ready for you back then.' His gaze held hers, his voice low. 'I'm not sure I'm ready for you now. But I know I want you. More than I've ever wanted any other woman before. And you want me too. I can see it in your eyes.' His hands slid to her neck, the roughened pads of his thumbs tilting her chin up. 'Feel it in your touch, in the way you tremble against me, like now. Why is it so hard for you to admit it?'

Ruby grabbed his wrists, unsure if she meant to dislodge his hold or press it closer. 'Because it doesn't make sense… Because nothing good can come from it… I don't know.' She shook her head. 'I can't think straight when you're this close to me. All my good sense seems to fly straight out the window.'

'Mine too.'

His lips came down over hers in a hard, hungry kiss that whispered of hot nights and silk sheets. A kiss that seduced and mastered at the same time as it tempted. Ruby sank into it, a low moan vibrating up from deep inside her. His tongue swept into her mouth, bold and confident, sending sensual sparks to every available nerve ending in her body. Her fingers forked into his thick hair, her body arching into his. This was what she wanted. What she craved.

'Yes,' he murmured, his hand rising to cup her breast, his thumb tracking over her aching nipple. 'Yes, Ruby, kiss me like that…just like that.'

Ruby quivered against him, her fingers slipping beneath the hem of his T-shirt to flatten against his taut abdomen. Her body hit sensual overload as the memory of how good it felt to have him inside her collided with the reality of dense, rock-hard muscle in the flesh.

At her quicksilver response the kiss grew even hotter, becoming more like a duel between two highly strung adversaries. A duel of competing desires. Punishing and claiming. Demanding and giving. Fierce, and yet sweetly tender at the same time.

Sam's hands on her body were sure and strong as they shaped her, his mouth sucking at her neck and making her skin pebble with greedy anticipation. Her own hands were busy learning his shape, working over his chest and revelling in the feel of all that taut, hot muscle.

'Sam—' Her voice broke as he bent and gently bit down on her nipple through her silk nightshirt, her body aching with a primal need that threatened to overtake her.

Sam muttered something under his breath, an oath, and then suddenly he was pushing her away.

'Dammit it, Ruby.' He held her at arm's length, his breathing as uneven as hers as he fought to get himself under control. 'I want you badly but I distinctly told you that the next time this happened it would be because you asked for it.'

Ruby blinked up at him, her passion-drugged senses taking longer to come online than his.

'Is that what you're doing?' he said gruffly. 'Are you asking me to kiss you? To make love to you?' He stabbed a hand through his hair. 'Because there's only one place this is headed, and if that's not what you want then you'd better let me know now while I still have self-control enough to stop.'

Ruby's lips felt swollen and tender, her nerves strung so tight they vibrated beneath the surface of her skin. She did want this. But she didn't. The conflicting desires made her feel as if she had a split personality. One telling her to go for it. The other telling her she was heading for a fall.

Sam shook his head, clearly reading her indecision for what it was. 'Don't bother answering that. It's written all over your face.'

'Where are you going?' she asked as he stalked away from her.

'To call a charter company to come and take you back to Sydney.' He looked at her over his shoulder. 'That is what you want, isn't it?'

He didn't wait for her answer and Ruby paced the large kitchen space, her bare feet slapping against the cool, hard tiles. What she wanted was about ten hours to pull herself together. And then another ten to give herself a stern talking-to. Her body still throbbed from where he had touched her, her legs as wobbly as an uncooked pudding.

She knew she was doing the right thing in not giving in to her desire for Sam, but that feeling was difficult to maintain when her heart went into over-drive every time he walked into a room. He was ev-erything she shouldn't want and did. And when she was in his arms she simply forgot that she worked for him and that he would walk away from her when he was done. She forgot that he got under her skin like no man before him and threatened everything she thought she knew about herself.

'When?' His harsh bark sounded loudly in the si-lent room. Ruby turned to see him stalking towards her, his phone to his ear. He stopped well short of her, his cool gaze holding hers as he listened to whoever was on the other end of the line, his strong thighs braced apart, muscles taut, a brooding scowl draw-ing his brows together. He looked like a walking advertisement for a gloriously pumped-up demigod in his prime.

Ruby's heart leapt inside her chest. The same giddy rush she had felt in his presence two years ago welled up inside her. 'When what?' she asked, her voice husky.

'When can you be ready to leave? Is thirty minutes too soon?'

Staring at his gorgeous, stony face, Ruby felt a surge of emotion and need swell inside her. The right thing to do, the *safe* thing to do, was to lock away all these feelings and tell him that she could be ready to go in five minutes, not thirty. But deep down she also knew that for the first time in her life she wanted something with an intensity that transcended the need for a safety net. She wanted him.

'Yes,' she answered, her lips dry as dust.

If possible his scowl deepened. 'How long, then?'

Before she could change her mind Ruby walked up to him and took the phone from his hand, putting it to her ear. 'Sorry,' she murmured, her eyes never leaving his. 'Prank call.' Then she depressed the End Call button and handed the device back to him, her breathing slightly ragged.

Sam stared at her, tension rolling off his big body and crashing into hers, making her insides quake.

Silence surrounded them, broken only by the soft sounds of Kong dreaming from his basket, and the rhythmic ticking of the wall clock.

'Be very sure, Ruby,' Sam said quietly, his voice rough and deep. 'My self-control isn't that good right now.'

Ruby moistened her lips, excited by the way Sam's dark gaze tracked the movement. It gave her a rush of feminine power to know that she turned on this highly charged male to such a degree. 'Neither is mine.'

Sam took a step that brought him right up against her and slowly drew her into his arms, his fingers tilting her chin up so that her eyes stayed locked on his. Heat poured off him, pressing against her body like sun-drenched stone. He was so tall and powerfully built she couldn't prevent the thrill of excitement that raced through her.

'No more denials?' he said fiercely.

'No.'

'And no more masks.'

'No.'

His hands shifted to her waist, rough and insistent as he lifted her so that her legs came up to wind around his waist.

'And no more pretending that this is about an itch any man can scratch.'

'Did it annoy you when I agreed with that?'

'Extremely,' he growled.

A thrill shot through her at the possessive note in his voice. 'Sam?'

'What?'

Ruby leaned forward and kissed the side of his neck the way he liked, breathing in his heady scent and revelling in the delirious taste of salt and man that was quintessentially Sam. 'Are you ever going to kiss me again?'

His smile was slow and lazy and promised passionate retribution for her impudence. 'Just waiting for you to ask me, Clarkson,' he murmured against her lips. 'Just waiting for you to ask.'

CHAPTER EIGHT

NOW THAT HE had her exactly where he wanted her, Sam felt his fingers tremble as he was gripped by a powerful emotion he couldn't name. It was deeper than anything he'd ever felt with a woman before and it nearly gave him pause. He knew this thing with Ruby was all-consuming but he was fairly certain he had a handle on it. Or was he only fooling himself?

Carrying her toward the bedroom, he bit down gently on the silky flesh of her earlobe, rewarded by her deep shudder and the quick, feminine hitch in her voice. She arched her neck to give him free licence to roam.

Of course he wasn't fooling himself. This thing, this incendiary chemistry between them, was just that. Chemistry and heat and—

'Dammit, Kong!' Sam cursed as he pushed open the door to the bedroom he'd used the night before and nearly tripped over the puppy that rushed in ahead of him. 'Sit!' he commanded, not caring if the pup obeyed him or not.

'Did he sit?' Ruby asked, nibbling his lower lip.

'Don't care,' he muttered. Her teasing ministrations had stripped away every vestige of sophistication he possessed and left a Cro-Magnon Man in his place. Still, he forced himself to slow down and lowered her to the centre of the bed. A row of tiny buttons split her nightshirt and Sam's gaze fastened on them, taking in the twin points of her hard nipples, which poked through the thin fabric. Unable to help himself, he lowered his head and captured one tight bud between his lips, bathing the cloth with his tongue.

A low moan escaped Ruby's lips and he glanced upward to find her lower lip caught between her teeth. 'You have beautiful breasts,' he murmured. 'So responsive.'

She shifted restlessly on the mattress, her fingers going to the top button of her shirt. Sam shook his head, straddling her and taking both her wrists in his hands and placing them on either side of her head. 'Let me,' he ordered roughly. 'I told you in the limo that I'd be taking my time when I finally got you horizontal. If you use those clever fingers on either one of us you'll destroy what little control I have left.'

She moistened her lips, heaving a sigh. 'There's no need to take your time. I'm so ready, Sam.'

Enjoying having her at his mercy, he bent over and licked the seam of her lips, moving back before she could tangle her tongue with his.

'Stop teasing,' she moaned.

'Oh, Clarkson,' he chuckled. 'I haven't even started yet.' But he was very afraid he wouldn't get to do everything he wanted to do because with every expanse of creamy skin he exposed he lost a little bit more of himself in the process. Knowing he should probably be a bit more worried about that, he couldn't bring himself to care. Especially when she was now naked save for a pair of panties emblazoned with the slogan Right Here, Right Now.

He quirked a brow in question.

Ruby gave a husky chuckle. 'Christmas gift from Molly. I wasn't expecting anyone else to see them.'

'Just make sure no one else does,' Sam growled, taking her mouth in a searing kiss that set them both to panting.

Working down the slender column of her throat, he shifted lower so that he could cup her breasts and admire the dusky-rose peaks. She arched up from the bed, her fingers kneading his waist and bunching his T-shirt high. Raising his head, he reefed it off over his head one-handed and groaned as her nails raked down over his torso and belly, covering his rigid length with the flat of her hand, his erection surging against the laces of his board shorts.

With growing urgency he trailed hot kisses over her collarbone, rubbing his stubbled jaw across one taut nipple and then the other before covering them in turn with his mouth, torturing her responsive flesh with his tongue and teeth before taking her deep into his mouth.

She moaned, arching higher off the bed, and Sam's hands went to her hips as he kissed lower. 'Much as I like these,' he murmured, shifting to the side and pulling her panties down her long legs, 'they have to come off.'

Smoothing a hand down her body he hooked one of her legs over his outer thigh and slid a hand down between their bodies to cup her silken curls. They were damp, the scent of her arousal turning him even harder as he parted her and stroked his fingers inside her silken heat.

She sobbed his name and need surged inside him. 'God, Ruby, you're beautiful.' Shifting lower, he urged her onto her back and held her thighs apart, kissing the backs of her knees before moving higher.

'Sam—' she gripped his hair, her fingernails digging into his scalp and sending goose pimples along his nape '—I need—'

'I know what you need.' He eased her thighs wider to fit his shoulders between them and touched his tongue to her tender flesh. She writhed beneath him and he had to anchor her hips to the bed with his forearm as he feasted on her honeyed centre, lapping at her and teasing her until she was keening and thrashing, and calling his name over and over.

He could tell she was close, her body shuddering and moving against him, and he quickened his movements, driving her higher, needing to hear her come for him, needing to feel it against his tongue. It had never been like this for him before. This deep-seated need to please a woman, to hear her soft cries of surrender as he pleasured her. And when finally she peaked it was the sweetest moment he could ever remember having.

Not giving her any time to recover, he crawled over her supine body and took her mouth in another drugging kiss. Despite his highly aroused body, it was almost enough: pleasuring her and having her come apart in his arms. But then her nimble fingers reached for the laces on his shorts and he knew she was as hungry to have him inside her as he was to be there.

Taking over the task, he reefed his shorts open and groaned in aching relief when her fingers circled him, gripping him in her tight fist. His eyes closed as she wriggled down the bed and replaced her fist with her mouth. He groaned again, forking his hand into her tumbling mass of hair as she used her lips and tongue to drive him as wild as he'd just driven her.

'Ruby, angel…' He lifted her upwards and rolled her beneath him. 'I need to be inside you,' he ground out, positioning himself between her thighs, widening them with his knees.

'Yes.' She gripped his face in her hands and brought his mouth down to hers as his body surged deep.

Then he swore. 'Condom,' he growled against her lips.

'I'm protected. Remember?' Her body rose to his and Sam bit back a groan as he sank further inside her tight sheath. Barely giving her time to adjust, he moved in her, filling her over and over with sure, deep strokes. It was as if his body belonged to some primitive part of himself he hadn't accessed before because he felt possessed. Possessed by some need to claim her and make her his.

'Relax, angel—you're so tight. Yes, God, yes, like that.'

He shuddered as her velvet heat clenched and released around his girth, her body milking his and emptying his brain of everything but her. Gripping her bottom in his hands, he angled her against him and drove even harder into her, urged on by her pleading little cries for more until in one fiery liquid moment they both hurled over the edge of reason and space and into the most satisfying release he had ever felt in his life.

He must have slept because at some point Ruby had snuggled into his arms. Or had he moved her there? Right now he didn't care because her feminine weight pressed up against him was all he could think about. Sensing that she was awake, Sam gently smoothed her hair back from her forehead. 'We finally made it to a bed,' he murmured, wondering if he had ever felt this sated before.

'Are you gloating?' she murmured sleepily.

'Not at all,' he said, knowing that was exactly what he was doing. 'I'm just relaying that I'm happy. Soft mattress. Soft sheets. Softer woman. What more can a man want?'

His stomach grumbled and Ruby blinked up at him, her gorgeous green eyes still slightly glazed from sleep.

'Food?' she suggested.

'Are you offering to fix me breakfast, angel?'

'Hmm, let me think about that.' Her eyes narrowed into threatening slits as she mock glowered at him. 'No.'

Sam laughed, reaching out to trace a finger down her cute, haughty nose. 'Well, if you're not going to fix me breakfast, what are you going to do for me?'

'Kick you out of bed,' she suggested sweetly. 'So you can fix me breakfast.'

Sam collapsed onto his back, taking her with him. 'After I've just serviced you like that?'

'Serviced me?' She lifted her head and her blonde hair cascaded like a waterfall of silk over one shoulder. Sam didn't bother resisting the temptation to thread his fingers through it. It was the most untidy he'd ever seen it and he loved the fact that he was responsible for mussing it. 'Serviced me?' she repeated. 'Like a horse?'

'Stallion.' He chuckled softly. 'Want me to do it again?'

Pink bloomed in her cheeks. 'Does it involve that thing you did with your tongue?'

'It might,' he promised, rolling over on top of her and covering her body with his. 'Did I hit the spot with that one?'

'Maybe…' she groaned as he smoothed her hair back and anchored her head for a hard, hungry kiss.

'You're insatiable,' she breathed, her hands roaming over the powerful slab of muscles that bisected his spine.

His lips tracked a path to her breast. 'With you I am,' he murmured, teasing the tip with his tongue.

'Sam…' Her voice trailed away as his lips fastened over hers once more, her hips angling upwards. Taking the invitation, Sam rolled her onto her stomach and stretched her hands high above her head.

'You okay with this?' he murmured against her ear.

'That depends on what this— Oh, yes. Yes. Definitely yes.' That last word was said on a long sigh as his thighs moved between hers and he entered her from behind. The contact was electrifying, wickedly good, and he had to grit his teeth to hold his orgasm at bay so she could reach hers first.

Coming back from that explosion of sensation wasn't easy, not even when Kong scratched at the door and barked urgently.

Ruby gave a half-moan, half-laugh. 'That's Kong.'

'No, it's the neighbour's dog,' Sam said, enjoying the sensation of having her beneath him, wrung out from the pleasure he'd just given her.

'In the bedroom?' She laughed, wriggling out from under him. 'I hope not. Sam—let me up—he must need to go out.'

Sam groaned and rolled onto his back. 'That dog has the worst timing in the world.'

'You're hungry, anyway,' she reminded him, scooting out of bed and grabbing his T-shirt off the floor.

He let his eyes travel over the long length of her before his T-shirt swallowed up the view. 'I know.'

'For food.' She gave him a stern look and reached for the door. 'Ah, I take back what I said.' She glanced at him over one shoulder. 'Kong doesn't need to go out. He's already left you a surprise.' Laughter lit her voice. 'Lucky for you, Miller and Valentino have floorboards.'

'Yeah, lucky for me,' Sam grumbled, not that he was truly upset. How could a man be upset on such a great day?

Somehow Sunday morning turned into Sunday evening, then Monday morning and now Monday afternoon. Neither she nor Sam had mentioned hiring a boat to return to Sydney, and when she'd called to ask after Miller's mother, she had blithely said that she and Sam had decided to stay at the beach house to discuss the big case they were working on.

She doubted Miller believed her, but she didn't push it. Maybe she could sense Ruby's emotional fragility down the end of the phone. Which, if she was honest, came and went depending on what they were doing.

If they were in bed together it was somehow nonexistent. Her mind, body and very essence were wholly taken up with Sam and everything they did to each other. There was no room for doubts when he laid his masterful hands on her body, expanding her sexual repertoire in ways that were utterly exhilarating.

If they were doing something casual like cooking together, or out walking Kong, taking in the bush setting and listening to the kookaburras herald that night was fast coming, then she felt a little more out of her depth.

Coming across the grand old beach house near Miller and Tino's, as they had done earlier that morning, had completely thrown her for a loop.

Having remembered Miller's comment that it was for sale, Sam had immediately wanted to investigate.

'I don't think we should,' she'd told him, trailing after him. 'It's private property.'

Sam had looked at her like a kid spying a Christmas tree. 'Where's your sense of adventure, Clarkson?'

'I lost it at law school,' she deadpanned, making him laugh.

'So what do you think?' he asked after peering into the downstairs windows.

'I love it.' She glanced at the peeling paint, and the overgrown vines spiralling out of control around the veranda posts. 'It's got so much character.'

'Want to buy it?'

'Me?' She laughed lightly, a sudden vision of her and Sam poring over paint samples and soft furnishings filling her head. 'Miller suggested you buy it so your future kids could all grow up together. I wasn't a part of that deal.'

She'd wandered away from him then, a bittersweet ache welling up in her chest. 'It looks like hard work,' she'd added, refusing to get caught up in the romance of the images that had taken hold and wouldn't let go. 'To make it beautiful again, I mean.'

Sam had come up behind her and slipped his arms around her waist. 'You should know by now that I don't mind hard work. Especially when it comes to beautiful things.'

Ruby had a strange feeling that he'd been talking about her and she'd blindly reached up to kiss him, replacing her intense emotional reaction with heat and need. He'd swiftly taken over the kiss and they'd barely made it back to Miller and Tino's house before he'd ravished her again.

Now, as they lay together under an ancient gum tree, the mid-afternoon sun dappling the lawn with interesting shapes while a few brave insects buzzed lazily in the heat, Ruby was trying not to go into full-on panic mode. Kong lay beside them, his fur slightly damp from where Sam had playfully hosed him down to help him cool off. They'd gone for a short run together along the beach, and the pup was exhausted from the effort.

Ruby turned her face up to the sun as she remembered fixing lunch together and making sweet, tender love afterwards. She barely recognised herself in Sam's presence. She couldn't remember the last time she'd felt this relaxed, and there wasn't a yoga pose in sight. Instead there was just him. Sam and his magic hands that knew just how to touch her, Sam with his gentle manner and infinite patience when he discovered Kong had treated his new shoe as a chew toy, and Sam with his intelligent conversation and broad, broad shoulders it would be so easy to lean on for a while.

Right from the beginning Sam had been able to strip away the guardedness she'd carried with her for ever, and sleeping with him, being like this with him, only seemed to make it harder to keep things in perspective. How much harder would it be if she actually fell in love with him?

In love with him?

This wasn't about love. Sam wouldn't want that from her and neither one of them had mentioned anything about emotions, or indeed, any of this going beyond the long weekend. In fact, Ruby knew that it couldn't go beyond the weekend because, regardless of what Sam thought, continuing to sleep together would definitely complicate their working life.

Ruby's heart thumped hard as her phone beeped a text message and, desperate for the distraction, she fished it out of her pocket as if it were a hundred-pound gold nugget she was trying to scratch out of the dirt.

'It's a text from my mother,' she said, sitting up so abruptly that Sam's fingers tangled in her hair.

Gently disentangling the strands, he scanned her face, which had grown pale as she read the long message.

'Something wrong?'

Ruby blinked, her brain trying to make sense of her mother's text. 'No. Yes. My mother is getting married!'

Sam looked at her, one arm behind his head, his brows knitted together as he watched her. 'You don't seem very happy about that.'

'I'm not. I mean, I am, but...' She shook her head. 'Honestly, I don't know what I feel.' Apart from agitated and unsettled. She jumped to her feet, instinctively needing to put space between her and Sam. 'My mother has this eternal optimism when it comes to relationships and it's so alien to me I find it hard to relate to.'

She paced over to the edge of the property and stared out at the bay beyond the trees. She felt Sam come up behind her, stiffening in case he tried to touch her.

'I don't follow.'

'My mother doesn't make very good decisions when she's in a relationship.' She turned towards him, hugging her arms over her stomach. 'She gets very needy and then it all goes wrong.'

'Is that what happened between her and your father?'

'In some ways.' She gave a hollow laugh. 'They used to fight all the time and sometimes it got so bad I would find Molly hiding under her bed and I'd read to her to help block it all out.' She glanced towards the bay again. 'I never understood it. My father never seemed happy and yet my mother had given up her career for him, which she later regretted when he left her for a work colleague.'

'That's tough.'

'It was. It took my mother a long time to recover and nothing I could ever say made her feel better about it.'

Sam frowned, his hands in his pockets as he watched her. 'Why was it your job to make her feel better about it? You were only a child.'

'I don't know. I think she became depressed and I was the only one available to help. Honestly, I would have done anything to make her happy back then.'

Sam gave her an astute look. 'So you were the rescuer of the family.'

'Rescuer?' Her short laugh was more an embarrassed cough. She couldn't believe that she'd just blurted out her family secrets like that. This weekend was about sex, not some lame therapy session. 'Hardly.' She made to move away from him but he stopped her, clasping her arms gently and drawing her resistant body closer.

'How old were you when your father left?'

'I was fourteen and—' She swallowed heavily, unsure how to switch topics without being obvious. 'It was the best thing really.' Apart from her mother going into a deep depression for a couple of years. 'Well, not the best, but it was certainly more peaceful after he left. Calmer. Only…'

'Only you missed him,' he finished for her, accurately interpreting the forlorn note in her voice.

'Yes.' She blinked back tears she hadn't realised had collected behind her eyes. 'Which is stupid because it probably wouldn't have worked out anyway.' She tried to smile to lighten the moment but her mouth wobbled and she ducked her head against Sam's shoulder. 'Why is love so difficult?'

'Because the human need for connection is so powerful, and sometimes you want that any way you can get it. Even if the other person doesn't want the same thing.'

Sensing that Sam was speaking from personal experience and more than ready to talk about something else, Ruby tilted her head back. 'Has that happened to you?'

'In a fashion.' His mouth twisted into a slight grimace. 'My old man was hardly ever around when I was growing up but that didn't change the way I felt about him.'

Ruby already knew from when Miller and Tino had got together that Sam's father had died in a fiery racing accident when Sam was young. 'Because he died, you mean?'

'No. He was unavailable long before that. He had his career and he didn't need much else.' *Certainly not him*, his tone implied. 'He was a larger-than-life figure who lived a life far removed from the real world.'

'Did you ever consider following him into racing like Valentino did?'

Sam laughed. 'Once. But I was told that I didn't have the reflexes for it so instead I concentrated on my studies. I decided if I couldn't impress him with my physical prowess, I'd do it academically. I should have known from watching my siblings that it wouldn't work. Not even Tino got our father's full attention and it was clear from early on that he had racing talent. I think it's fair to say that my father wasn't very family-oriented.'

Ruby had had no idea that they shared the similar experience of having emotionally distant fathers and her arms instinctively went around his waist to offer comfort. 'I'm sorry, Sam. I didn't know.'

'Why would you?' He smoothed her hair back from her forehead. 'But the past is the past. You can't change it. You just deal with it and get over it.'

'Do you?' she asked, thinking about herself as much as Sam. 'Do you get over it or does it change you in ways you can't reverse?' Because love wasn't something she'd ever trusted and she didn't know how to get around that. Or even if she wanted to.

'Who knows?' he said, scooping her into his arms so suddenly she squealed.

Kong barked, dancing around Sam's feet as he sensed the rising excitement between them.

'What are you doing?' Ruby clung to Sam's neck.

'You'll find out.'

'Sam?' She spied the sparkling swimming pool with dubious delight. 'I'm not wearing a swimsuit.'

Sam grinned down at her, his gaze hot. 'Neither am I.'

Kong scratched at the bedroom door later that afternoon and Sam buried his head beneath the pillows.

'That dog is going back to the rescue centre as soon as we get back to Sydney,' he grumbled.

Ruby stirred beside him and planted a kiss on his shoulder. 'No, he's not. You love him too much to give him back. But stay here. I'll let him out this time.'

Sam rolled over and snatched her close against him before she got very far. 'Can you bring back my phone? I should check when Tino is picking us up later on this evening. Not that I want the weekend to end.'

'All good things come to an end,' she murmured, wriggling out of his arms and throwing on his T-shirt.

Closing his eyes, Sam wondered about her last comment. Was Ruby right? Did all good things have to come to an end or could they go on endlessly? Before he could conjure up an answer Ruby flew back into the room.

'Oh, my God, you have to get up. Valentino is here.'

'Already?'

'Yes, it's five o'clock in the afternoon, and I think he saw me.'

Sam's gaze drifted down over her figure, clad in another one of his T-shirts and nothing else. They hit her mid-thigh and had become her weekend wear because they were so easy to remove. 'That could be a problem.' His eyes turned heavy-lidded. 'I'll have to kill him if he saw anything.'

'Stop joking around. You have to get up. Get dressed.'

Sam yawned, not seeing the problem. After making love and talking for most of the day he was completely sated.

Not that they'd talked about anything important. Like what would happen once they returned to Sydney. He'd thought about it after Ruby had fallen asleep earlier on and he knew he wanted things to continue between them once they got back. No doubt she would see it as a complication but it didn't have to be. The truth was he liked her. He liked spending time with her in bed and out, he liked her sass and her fire, he liked her professional confidence and the way she pushed herself and others to help those in need.

His gaze softened as he watched her searching for something under the bed. He especially liked seeing her laugh when his dog slobbered all over her face, and he loved her skyscraper-shoe collection. Why would he want to give that up and move on before he was ready?

'Sam! You're still in bed!'

Seeing her panic, Sam wondered if he shouldn't be doing the same thing. Certainly he hadn't been overly comfortable disclosing his feelings about his father as he'd done earlier, but then he hadn't been nearly as uncomfortable as she had been talking about hers. He wondered if he shouldn't be more alarmed about how much he had shared with her, and then became distracted by her sweet curves.

'Calm down,' he said in a reassuring tone. 'Tino already knows you're here.'

Kong barked at the door and Ruby nearly jumped out of her skin. 'Yes, but he doesn't know I'm here like this—with you! He thinks we're working on a case.'

'So what? He'll figure it out in time.'

'I don't want him to figure it out. If someone at the office should find out…' She left the rest of the sentence hanging but Sam got the general gist and didn't like it. He rolled out of bed and yanked on his board shorts, trying not to become irritated. 'My brother isn't indiscreet and last time I checked he didn't work for me.'

'I still don't want him or Miller to know about…' Her hand waved between them as if she was at a loss for words, and that infuriated him even more. 'I mean, one night at a party is explainable—sort of. But this…'

'This?' Sam wondered how his voice remained so calm when his head felt as if it might explode.

'This weekend.' She angled her stubborn chin higher. 'It's between us and no one else.'

'Let me get this straight.' Sam stalked towards her, a dangerous smile on his face. 'You want me to be your dirty little secret going forward, is that it?'

She frowned. 'No, that's not—'

'Good.' He tunnelled his fingers into her hair and tilted her face up for a hard, brief kiss. 'Because I don't operate that way.'

* * *

But in the end he had operated that way. He'd closed Valentino's curious glance down with just a look and carried their bags onto the yacht. Fortunately his brother wasn't a stupid man and had taken the hint, making small talk to fill the lengthening silence.

Apparently he'd sent Sam a text that morning informing him that he'd collect both him and Ruby a little earlier than planned, which Sam would have known if he'd bothered to check his phone. As it was a public holiday, he hadn't seen the need. And he'd been too busy. Too busy making love with Ruby and catching up on sleep he hadn't got the night before.

A tight sensation settled in his chest as the yacht skimmed over the increasingly choppy waves. He could only ever remember wanting one other thing as much as he wanted this woman. Back then his father had been out of reach. Ruby wasn't. *Was she?*

And what exactly did he want from her?

He brooded over the question as he watched her. He might not know exactly what he did want, but he knew what he didn't—and that was for her to continue to treat him like a leper after the weekend they'd just indulged in.

He scowled as the yacht finally steered a course into the brilliantly bejewelled Sydney Harbour. The wind whipped Ruby's hair back as her face lifted to the bright sunshine and the tight sensation worsened. They'd barely exchanged two words since Valentino had picked them up. Instead Ruby had questioned his brother about how Miller's mother was, and whether or not she needed anything; basically acting as if she hadn't spent the last two days coming apart in his arms.

What she hadn't done was follow the normal trajectory he was used to, where a woman expected more from him than he was prepared to give, and subtly tried to question him about what happened next.

Irritated because the one woman he *did* want to expect more from him actually *didn't*, Sam strode from the yacht after Tino docked, growling at Ruby as she accepted Tino's offer of a lift home, firmly directing her to his own jeep and driving her home himself.

She didn't say anything on the way, petting Kong and staring at the Sydney landscape she'd seen a million times before. Needing to work out his own agenda, Sam had left her to her thoughts, but now, as he pulled up outside her apartment block, he knew he had to say something.

Moving Kong to the back seat, he went around to open Ruby's door, barely restraining his irritation when he found her already waiting for him on the kerb.

'I'll walk you up,' he clipped out, reaching for her bag.

'No need,' she said clasping the handle as if it were full of jewels and she was staring at a newly released prison inmate. 'I had a lovely time this weekend. Thank you.'

Sam ground his teeth together. 'This isn't exactly the way I planned for it to end, Ruby.'

'It was a little awkward with Valentino turning up like that but—'

'I'm not talking about my brother. I'm talking about you and me.' His voice was deep, rough. 'Spend the night with me.' He placed his hands on her shoulders. 'Come back to my place and let me fix you dinner.'

'I can't.' She wouldn't meet his eyes. 'I have to look over work stuff and—'

'Do it at mine.'

'Molly expects me home. We agreed to talk about Mum's situation.'

'Her wedding, you mean.'

'Yes.' He could feel the tension emanating from the tight muscles in her shoulders and wanted to ease the burden she felt. 'Your mother is a big girl, Ruby. She can take care of herself.'

'I know that.' She pulled back from him and he knew he'd offended her. 'I'm not an idiot.'

'I didn't say you were.'

Frustrated, Sam dragged a hand through his hair. The more Ruby tried to put walls up between them, the more he wanted to tear them down. 'I'm only trying to offer you support.'

'I don't need your support, Sam. I'm a big girl as well.'

'Dammit, would you stop being so prickly?' His hands slid down to her hips and he tugged her closer.

'I don't want to argue with you. I want to see you again.'

Her head went back as she frowned. 'Sorry?'

'Did you seriously think one weekend is all I would want?'

'Yes. No! I don't know.'

'Well, it's not,' he said gruffly. 'I want more.'

'How much more?' she asked huskily.

'I don't know,' he answered honestly. 'But I do know I don't want this to end yet.'

Ruby bit into her lower lip, her fingers turning the front of his T-shirt into a piano accordion.

'What about you?' His voice sounded rough. 'What do you want?'

'I don't know either,' she said hesitantly. 'We work together and—'

'That's a real sticking point for you, I know.' He stared down at her. 'So, okay, lay it on me.'

'What?' she asked warily.

'Some scenarios.'

'Scenarios?'

'Imagined situations you think are going to go wrong in the future.' He flashed her a grin. 'You can start with your biggest fear.'

Her eyes flew wide as if to say that there was no way she would be starting with her biggest fear. 'So you can shoot it down?'

'Of course.' His grin widened. 'Come on, Clarkson—I'm good at this, trust me.'

'Fine.' She drew in a deep breath. 'If we continue

this and someone at the office finds out the gossip would be hideous.'

'The only way anyone at work can find out is if one of us is indiscreet and talks. I'm not going to do that, and I doubt you are either.'

'You could become uncomfortable seeing me in the office every day and change your mind about mixing business with pleasure.'

'And fire you presumably?'

Ruby raised a brow at his cavalier tone. 'It's been done before. And you are my boss.'

'True. But I'm not that small-minded.'

'What happens if one of us decides to end things?'

'We behave like mature adults and go on as normal.' He gave her a slow grin and tugged her closer. 'Anything else?'

'I'm sure there is but I can't think of it right now.'

'Because you're creating mountains where there are none.' He leant in and kissed her. 'Say yes.'

'Sam.' She groaned against his lips, her arms tight around his neck. 'I think you could wear down a Sherman tank just by looking at it.'

Sam frowned. 'I don't want to wear you down.' Was she saying that she didn't want this? That she didn't want *him*? It felt like a sharp blade had just been rammed through his midsection. 'If this isn't what you want then just say the word and I'll walk away right now.' Even if it seemed impossible to do so. 'Is that what you want, Ruby—do you want me to walk away?'

'No.' The word was barely a whisper but it kick-started his heart again. 'I don't want you to walk away, Sam, but I'm not very good at this. I don't know how to make it work.'

The words rushed out of her as if she was taking an enormous risk just saying them. The echoes of that feeling resonated somewhere deep inside Sam as well. 'You make it work one step at a time,' he said gently. 'At the office we keep things to business as usual, and on the weekends...' He gave her a slow smile and slipped his hands into her hair. 'On the weekends we burn up the sheets together until we can't move. How does that sound?'

'Like trouble,' she said, pressing closer. 'But okay, if we do this we have to keep it simple.'

'Very simple.'

Ruby nodded so seriously Sam had to pull back from kissing her again. 'No unnecessary promises and no repercussions,' she pressed.

'None.'

'And no emotional entanglements. From either one of us.'

The light breeze swept a few strands of hair across her face. Sam pushed them back. 'Ever do anything without a caveat, Clarkson?'

'Not usually,' she grumbled reluctantly. 'Is that a problem?'

'No, my crazy little control freak, it's not.'

'I am not a—'

'You are and I love it.' He crushed her lips beneath

his in a greedy kiss, only coming up for air when they were both breathless and wanting.

'Feel what you do to me, Ruby. What we do to each other.' He ran the pad of his thumb across her lower lip, soothing her swollen flesh. 'What have you got to lose by saying yes?'

Her eyes were heavy-lidded with a desire he knew was reflected in his own. 'Nothing,' she whispered.

But what Sam heard in her voice, what he *felt* when she tightened her arms around his neck, was *everything*. And he didn't know if he was the one thinking that, or she was.

CHAPTER NINE

ON THEIR NEXT weekend together they flew to Melbourne, hired a car and drove along the rugged cliffs of the Great Ocean Road.

Victoria wasn't as warm as New South Wales, so Sam had stopped at a local market and bought her a shawl to wrap herself in. They'd stayed in a gorgeous house overlooking the sea in Apollo Bay, lit an open fire in the hearth and toasted marshmallows, talking about everything from horror exam days at university to the merits of the government's new environmental-law package, and favourite Broadway musicals—none in Sam's case, loads in hers.

Ruby found out that Sam had gone into law because his father was usually scathing about it, and she'd told him how she had an over-developed sense of fairness that drove her to want to set things right.

The following weekend Sam had flown them to Far North Queensland, where they'd stayed in an eco-resort and snorkelled with dolphins, and slept out under the stars. Kong had gone with them on both trips, proving to be an excellent travelling companion apart from the sofa leg he had chewed at the house in Apollo Bay, and which Sam had already replaced with a more expensive version.

When both Molly and Miller had asked where she was going she had made up some new, top-secret case that she had to oversee, and, although they had looked suspicious, they were used to her working over weekends, so it wasn't that much of a stretch for them to believe her.

That had been two weeks ago and since then Ruby had hardly seen, or heard from, Sam. Mainly that was due to Drew and Mandy having had their baby, a beautiful little girl, which had caused Sam's responsibilities to double. Then last week he'd had to fly to LA when an old case he'd been working on had blown up. He'd been sorry to cancel yet another weekend together but he'd had no choice.

He'd even thanked her for taking it so well, but what had he expected? That she would get clingy? Ruby didn't do clingy. Ever.

And really, Sam's being away had been a good thing. Her own caseload had significantly increased since the merger and she'd needed a lot of uninterrupted time to get on top of it.

She'd also used her free weekend to catch up with her mother and Phil, the fiancé.

They'd lunched at a chic French bistro on the previous Sunday, and her mother had been delighted to fill her in on the story of their romance.

Apparently theirs had been a whirlwind affair—

her mother's favourite kind—and Ruby only hoped this one would last longer than the many others over the years. Though, to be fair, none of the others had made it to the engagement stage. It still surprised Ruby that after her father had walked out, leaving her mother shocked and devastated, she was optimistic enough to date as often as she had and to even try marriage again. But she had to admit that her mother did seem happy with Phil, and that was all Ruby had ever wished for her.

With Sam's sage words in her ear—words she hadn't wanted to hear at the time—about her mother being a big girl and able to take care of herself, Ruby found herself biting her tongue rather than warning her mother to be careful. Of course, she didn't think that her behaviour was *that* different from the norm, but Molly had frowned at her after the lunch and asked if she was okay.

'Fine,' she'd said blithely. 'I've just decided to stop trying to save Mum when it's obvious she doesn't want, or need, that from me any more.'

Molly gaped at her. 'Okay, where's my sister and how much do you want for her return?'

At the time Ruby had given her *that* look, but deep down she wondered the same thing. She did feel different at times—looser and less worried about everything, and always wondering what Sam was doing. Like now, for instance, when she should be preparing for a major meeting with Carter Jones she was actually working out the time difference in LA.

And every time she wondered if she was being a bit naive in agreeing to see Sam past that long weekend at the beach house, every time she wondered if she wasn't getting in a little over her head, her body would pulse with remembered longing and she couldn't bring herself to end it.

Yet.

But what was he doing now? Working, as he had said, or was he catching up with friends? Had he run into an old flame? Was his lack of contact a signal that he was already tiring of their relationship? Ruby's stomach bottomed out. Had the time they had spent together been enough for him, while for her the more time she spent with him, the more she *wanted* to spend with him?

It took everything in her not to get uptight or paranoid, and she felt as if she'd succeeded right up until she heard his voice outside her office coming down the hallway.

'That's great news. Have their CFO call me. Those contract negotiations can get tricky when you least expect it, so she needs to be fully briefed ahead of time.'

Ruby only had a moment to collect herself before Sam was standing, larger than life, in her doorway, so handsome it hurt her heart to look at him.

Grant muttered a greeting, barely looking up from his computer, his fingers working furiously on the contract they were planning to put to Carter Jones in less than two hours' time.

Leaving Grant to it, she smiled at Sam, only to find his expression so serious a lump formed in her throat. He *had* met someone in LA. Someone at a party, he was sorry, but what could he do? It was back to business as usual for them.

'I've just heard that Jones has called a mediation meeting for this afternoon,' he said, his dark eyes holding hers. 'Are we ready for it?'

Quickly shifting gear from the personal to the professional, and hating the sick, insecure feeling clawing at her stomach, Ruby exhaled slowly. 'Yes. He's panicking because of the media leak last week, and also because we've refiled a motion with the court for a class action suit. He's also no doubt wanting to capitalise on the fact that the mobile phone videos we have showing his managers browbeating their employees will likely be inadmissible in court.'

'Move in for the kill while he assumes we're hurting more than he is,' Sam suggested.

'Yes.'

Nodding, Sam glanced at his mobile phone. 'I've cleared my diary for the next few hours. What time are you both leaving for his office?'

He'd cleared his diary? Ruby hadn't even known he was back in the country. He hadn't sent her a single text since asking how her afternoon went with her mother on Sunday. God, she hoped he didn't sense how off-balance she felt right now.

'An hour.'

Holding her gaze, Sam spoke to Grant. 'Give us a minute, would you, Grant?'

It wasn't a request and Grant didn't take it as one, balancing his open laptop in his arms as he left them alone.

Sam closed the door behind him and Ruby's throat bobbed as she swallowed. 'Was there something else?'

Sam came towards her, rounding her desk in three easy strides. 'Yes.' He pulled her to her feet, his eyes searching hers. 'I've missed you.'

Stunned, Ruby could only stare up at him. She'd slipped her shoes off under her desk, so she felt tiny as he towered over her, his dark, hot eyes pinning her to the spot. Her heart was beating so hard inside her chest she'd be surprised if he couldn't hear it as clearly as she could.

'You've got exactly two seconds to tell me no before I kiss you,' he murmured gruffly.

'I…' She moistened her lips, utterly intoxicated by the heady rush at having all that power and strength completely focused on her.

'One.' He stepped forward.

'We shouldn't.'

He took another step, his gaze on her mouth. 'That's not a no. Two.'

Not realising that he'd backed her against the wall until she felt its solid presence behind her, she flattened her hands against his hard chest. She knew if she told him to back off that he would. In a second.

She didn't want him to. Instead she slid her hands to his shoulders and moaned his name as his mouth crashed down over hers.

The kiss was delicious. Deep and drugging. Sam's rough growl and powerful body letting her know just how much he wanted her. Ruby went liquid.

At that point she wouldn't have cared if Drew and his father, and the whole executive team, were crowded into the room taking notes. She'd missed Sam more than she wanted to admit and it was heaven to be in his arms again. To be touching him again.

Fortunately Sam did care, easing back to rest his forehead against hers. When he felt her legs take her weight once more he released her and took a step back. 'Sorry. I know that crossed your line, but the last two weeks have been interminable. Have dinner with me tonight.'

'Okay.' It wasn't the weekend but she couldn't have cared. 'Oh, no! I can't. I promised Molly I'd run through lines with her tonight. She has a big audition coming up.'

'How long will that take?'

'Not all night.'

His smile was slow and full of sensual promise just as Veronica hurried in carrying a packing box. 'I just found this in— Oh, sorry, I didn't realise you had someone with you.'

'I was just leaving,' Sam said smoothly. 'Tonight,' he added before leaving them.

Veronica set the box on Ruby's desk. 'I finally located your missing books.' She started unpacking them. 'So what's on tonight?'

'Nothing…' Ruby surreptitiously smoothed the corners of her mouth, thankful that she hadn't reapplied her lipstick after lunch. 'Just a…a work thing.'

'Oh, okay.' Veronica gave her an enigmatic smile as she retreated to answer the ringing phone on her desk. 'Well, enjoy your *work thing* and don't forget your shoes this time.'

Ruby groaned. She hadn't fooled Veronica one bit. She closed her laptop and slipped on her heels, a small smile tilting her lips. Probably she should feel a bit more worried about that. And maybe she would if her body wasn't still buzzing from that kiss.

By the time they reconnected in the car that whisked them to the Star Burger building, Ruby was glad to have Grant along for the ride. She was a bag of nerves and she knew that was only because Sam was with them. Usually, she felt completely in charge by this stage of the proceedings, knowing that her preparation was rock-solid in the cases she worked on. Now, though, there was so much at stake and part of that was impressing Sam, which should not have been uppermost in her mind.

Pulling herself together, she flipped the switch on her emotions and focused on what she had to accomplish as the three of them strode into Carter Jones's palatial suite of offices. After they were left cooling their heels for ten minutes Sam quietly informed the snooty receptionist that he would walk out and terminate all future negotiations with the restaurant giant if they were left to wait a second longer.

Miraculously, Carter's personal assistant arrived—a woman who looked as if she'd stepped from the pages of *Glamour* magazine—and escorted them to a richly designed conference room.

Two minutes later Carter Jones, a large, balding man with bulging eyes strode in, flanked by Tom Roberts, his head lawyer, and six minions. Ruby knew of Tom's reputation as a corporate shark and had little time for the man, who was as unscrupulous as he was smart. She didn't bother to return his superior smile and nor did Sam or Grant.

Carter didn't smile at all, glaring across the table at her and saying nothing, while Tom shuffled papers and started his opening pitch. Which was basically 'we won't pay and you don't have a case'.

'Please tell me you didn't call us all the way down here just to go over old ground, Tom,' Ruby said pleasantly. Having had him blustering on the phone to her on more than one occasion last week, she really wanted to close this case, not drag it out.

Tom's mouth turned down at the corners. 'We know you're wanting to get local MP Tessa Miles involved to support your evidence—or lack thereof— but she won't go on the stand, Ruby. You're following a dead dodo with that one.'

Ruby gave him a cool look. 'I'd recheck my information if I were you, Tom. Not only will Ms Miles go on the stand, but she's already provided us with her written testimony. And yes, it is signed.'

That got Tom's attention, and while he conversed with one of his minions Carter Jones stared down his nose at her, dismissing her out of hand before eye-balling Sam. 'Who's running this dud outfit, Ventura? You or your subordinate?'

'Don't mind me,' Sam said, 'I'm just window-dressing on this one.'

Carter tossed a mint into his mouth and chewed noisily. 'You can't win this case, Ms Clarkson. Those little videos you're so proud of will be deemed inad-missible in court.'

'Quite possibly,' Ruby agreed, 'but, with Ms Miles's testimony and more potential clients contacting our office because of the recent media storm, we don't need them.'

'What other potential clients?' Tom asked, chok-ing on his water.

'Didn't you get my memo, Tom? You might want to check with your staff. We should be up to fifty by the time we get back to the office.'

Unsure whether to believe her or not, Tom stood up, sprouting reams of legal precedents and inade-quate documentation until Carter snarled at him. 'Sit the hell down and shut the hell up. You've been com-pletely useless on this case from day one, Roberts.'

Tom turned crimson under the weight of Cart-er's frog-like glare, his fellow lawyers shifting uneasily in their seats. Ruby almost felt sorry for the man. Almost.

'All right, how much do those hungry little bloodsuckers want from me?' Carter all but spat at her.

'Carter, I think we should take a moment to consider our options,' Tom suggested quietly.

'Take all day,' Sam drawled. 'It won't change anything.'

'I don't need a moment,' Carter barked. 'Give me a figure.'

Ruby named a fairly meagre sum that their clients had agreed upon, even though she had informed them that they were due a lot more.

'Is that all?' Carter Jones laughed incredulously. 'You mean to tell me that I've been fighting this dog of a case for a pittance? I'll accept your resignation forthwith, Roberts.'

'That's not all we want,' Ruby added softly.

Carter's bull neck swivelled to meet her direct gaze. 'We also want you to make a yearly donation to refugee centres around the country.' She named a figure and this time it was much more substantial.

Carter gave a hacking cough. 'You're pushing your luck, lady.' He passed his gaze to Sam. 'You going to just sit there and let her get away with this, Ventura?'

'And a public apology,' Ruby continued as if he hadn't spoken. 'In writing to each and every plaintiff.'

Carter's thin lips were pressed so tightly together they looked like a jagged surgical scar. 'No deal.'

'I was hoping you'd say that.' Ruby smiled. 'I can't wait to meet you in court, Mr Jones.'

'Fine. I'll do what you want.' A thick white line of spittle collected at the corner of Carter's mouth as he called her a derogatory name under his breath.

'You call my associate that again—' Sam said with such lethal softness it was scarier than waiting for a bomb to go off '—you and I will have a talk in a closed room.'

Carter's beetle-like gaze sharpened as it moved between her and Sam, and Ruby felt her face turn pink as his upper lip curled unpleasantly. 'Like that, is it?'

'It's not like anything,' she interjected forcefully, knowing immediately that she should have kept her big mouth closed.

Carter started to laugh and Sam cut him off with a look.

'We'll have the contract on your desk within the hour,' he said, taking over while Ruby could do nothing but inwardly curse her own ineptitude.

'It's in his inbox as we speak,' Grant murmured, typing on his computer.

'Dipping the wick a bit close to home, aren't you, Ventura?' Carter said snidely.

Having finally pulled herself together, Ruby gave Carter a quelling look. 'You keep going, Mr Jones, and you'll have a defamation suit launched against you as well as a class action. If that's all, gentlemen—' she cast a glance around the room '—we'll be on our way. Sorry you lost your job, Tom.'

Physically vibrating with tension, Ruby thought she might snap in half as the three of them entered the lift and pressed the button for the ground floor.

'I think we just won,' Grant ventured softly into the heavy silence.

They had, but Ruby was still so fired up on humiliation at Carter Jones's slur that she couldn't even bring herself to enjoy it. There was no way she could bring a defamation case against him because what he had said was true.

'Ruby—'

'I'm fine, Sam,' she said, wanting to shut him down so that she could deal with her emotions alone.

Unaware of the tension radiating between the two of them, Grant shook his head as if he was coming out of a long daze.

'I can't believe Jones caved in like that. Well, I can, but...' He cut Ruby a curious look. 'What was with the fifty extra potential clients? I thought we'd only picked up one more.'

'I might have embellished a bit with that,' Ruby admitted with a half smile.

'Genius,' Grant murmured as they stepped out into the solid wall of the oppressive Sydney humidity. 'You are officially my new hero, Ms Clarkson. So?' He gave them both a broad grin. 'Drinks at Mickey Dee's? I'd say we've earned it after that.'

Going to their local haunt was the last thing Ruby felt like doing. So much harder to hide and lick her wounds in a public space. 'Not for me,' she said.

'I'm going back to the office to call our clients and let them know the outcome.'

'Sorry. I also need to return to the office,' Sam said, opening the back door to the limousine and waiting for Grant to move inside before subtly blocking Ruby's way with his body.

'I can tell you're going to be irrational about this,' he murmured so that only she could hear. 'But I would have defended any one of my colleagues in exactly the same way.'

Ruby kept her gaze level with the top of the car. It wasn't so much Sam's defence of her that had upset her; it was her own reaction in giving herself away that bothered her. 'I said I was fine.'

When he didn't immediately move out of her way she glanced up to find him frowning. 'Forget Carter Jones and concentrate on the fact that you did a brilliant job in there. You do a brilliant job full stop.'

'Thanks.' She felt emotion well up in her throat, clogging it.

Oh, God, she couldn't do this. She couldn't be with Sam and not because of work, or her reputation, and not because Veronica had guessed there was something going on between them or because Carter Jones had been crude, but because she had fallen in love with him.

Completely and irrevocably.

An incontrovertible mistake, given that they were only having an affair. An affair she knew would end at some point. Leaving her crushed.

The knowledge slid into place inside her with the ease of a softball player sliding into home plate—followed swiftly by a tide of rising panic.

Finally Sam inclined his head and moved out of her way. 'You're not okay, but we'll discuss it tonight.'

Would they? Ruby was already wondering how she would be able to get out of seeing him. She was so far out of her comfort zone right now she'd need the Hubble space telescope to find it.

And what she needed more than seeing Sam was distance. Distance to work out how she had gone from great, casual sex to love when she'd been so careful to avoid it.

Back in his office Sam ran a frustrated hand through his hair.

He knew Ruby was upset with the not so subtle threat he'd made to Jones in their meeting but, dammit, she was being unreasonable about that. Sam was used to defending people; it was what he did. No hesitation. No sign of weakness. His father had hated weakness. 'If you hesitate, you lose—it's that simple,' he'd used to say.

Sam had taken the mantra to heart—at first to try and please his father, but after that he'd seen that it worked. But Ruby saw his methods as—what had she said?—being like a Sherman tank. Was that the problem? Was that what she'd reacted to so strongly? Well, he couldn't say he wouldn't do it again. That would be a lie. No one insulted his woman and got away with it. Ever.

His woman…

He knew that was what she was even if she didn't yet. The realisation had hit him hard the night before when he'd been at a work dinner in LA. As usual he'd been thinking about her, wondering what she was up to, and whether or not he should call her, when the woman beside him had placed her hand on his knee beneath the table. Sam had been so surprised he hadn't reacted immediately. When he had it was to lean in close and tell her that he was taken. She'd pouted up at him, looking at him from beneath her lashes, and asked if he'd been sure, and he'd said, 'Unequivocally.' And he was.

Meeting Ruby had knocked him on his backside two years ago and he'd been slowly sliding into love ever since. That night at the Herzog party had sealed his fate, if he had only known it then, but now that he did he couldn't imagine being with anyone else.

And he was pretty sure she felt the same way about him.

He glanced up as Wilma, the secretary he'd inherited from Mr Kent Senior, knocked and entered his office. 'I thought you'd left for the night,' he said.

'Nearly, Mr Ventura. I just have a few things to tidy up before I go.'

He smiled at her, absently wondering how Tino had first told Miller how he felt. Had he come straight out and said that he loved her, or had he done it with flowers? Serenaded her over a candlelit dinner? Should he organise flowers to fill the grand old beach house he'd just purchased beside Miller and Tino's? Get someone to deliver a meal there, set up a few candles and maybe attach a note to Kong's collar? Hadn't a woman he once dated told him she'd seen it on the internet and it was the cutest move ever?

'Mr Ventura? Sir?'

Realising he'd completely zoned out, Sam gave Wilma a quick smile. 'Sorry, Wilma. What have you got for me?'

'A couple of letters to go into tonight's post.'

No, he wouldn't use his dog, but he would do it at the new beach house. He'd organise dinner and candles. Maybe some soft music... Or was that overkill?

A frown formed on his face. Why was the idea of telling a woman he loved her and wanted to marry her so difficult? Because that was the other part of this: he wanted to marry Ruby and spend the rest of his life with her.

'Is there something wrong with the letter, sir?'

Letter?

Sam stared at the pieces of paper he hadn't even realised he was holding. He blew out a controlled breath. 'No, Wilma, nothing.'

Scanning the contents, he quickly scrawled his signature across the bottom of both letters and handed them back. 'Anything else?'

'The Cutter brief you wanted me to change, and some interoffice transfer documents. Congratulations, by the way, on winning the Star Burger case. The office is buzzing with the news. We're going to miss Ruby when she's gone.'

'Thanks.' Sam took the Cutter brief, planning to review it at a later— 'Gone?' He glanced up at Wilma. 'Gone where?'

'The London office, sir.'

'Ruby. As in *my* Ruby?'

'Well, that's a very nice way to put it, sir. Yes, your Ruby.' She beamed him a smile. 'I have her and Stephen Price's transfer documents for you to sign off on. I know it's all done on computer nowadays but Mr Kent Senior liked to keep a paper copy of staff changes so that he was always aware of who went where. It harks back to the days when the firm was the size of a corner shop.' She gave him a small laugh. 'I wasn't sure of your preference, so I erred on the side of caution.'

A terrible coldness settled over Sam. He took the remaining papers Wilma offered and stared down at Ruby's transfer document without really seeing it. 'Did Ruby apply for this or did London request the transfer?'

'I'm sorry, sir, I couldn't say, but if you like I can— Mr Ventura? Sir? Is something wrong?'

Yes, there was something wrong, Sam thought grimly as he strode out of his office. *There was something very wrong.*

Ruby's secretary gave him a startled glance as he approached her desk.

'She in?'

'Yes, she is. She's—'

Sam didn't wait to hear the rest, pushing the door to Ruby's office wide open even as he told himself to calm down.

Not that it did any good. He'd never felt more blindsided by anything in his life.

Ruby stopped pacing as soon as Sam burst into her office, her heart doing that little quickstep it always did when she saw him.

'We need to talk.'

Her eyes raked his face. He was looking at her as if she'd committed a crime, every well-honed muscle in his body drawn tight. Was he here to discuss her response to his threat to Carter Jones? She had already decided that she might have overreacted a little in the meeting, but she was nowhere near ready to discuss the reason behind it.

Equally he could be looking all dark and foreboding because something had gone wrong with the deal. It wouldn't surprise her at all if Carter had tried to renege on the agreement he had made after the fact, and she inwardly cringed again at how easily she assumed Sam would be in her office for personal reasons rather than professional ones.

'What's wrong?' she asked, deciding that he must be here because of Carter Jones. 'Has something changed in the Star Burger decision?'

'Not to my knowledge.' His tone was clipped,

cold. It made her shiver. 'Wilma just gave me this to sign.'

He handed her a document and it took Ruby a moment to realise it was her interoffice transfer request. She hadn't realised that HR had approved it.

'When were you going to tell me about it?'

Startled by his harsh tone, Ruby frowned. 'I don't know. I hadn't given it much thought.' In fact, she hadn't given it any thought. She'd been so busy and so preoccupied lately she'd completely forgotten she'd even applied for it. God, she really was a mess.

'You hadn't given it much thought?' He shook his head, his frown deepening. 'You applied for it, didn't you?'

'Well, yes, but...' She had only applied because she didn't think they'd be able to work together and since then she'd had other things on her mind. Things like what they would do together on the weekends, and whom he was with when he wasn't with her. Things that were all embarrassing indications that yet again she had regressed to the emotional maturity of an insecure schoolgirl where Sam was concerned. 'Is that a problem?'

If possible his expression turned even darker. 'What kind of a question is that? Of course it's a damn problem.'

Ruby moistened her lips. 'I'm usually pretty good at remembering things. I'm sorry—I guess I've been busy.'

'Too busy to let me know that you're moving to London?'

'Well, I wasn't sure if it would even be approved and—'

'And you thought you'd wait, is that it? Spring it on me at the last minute?'

'No.' She frowned as she tried to make sense of his mocking tone. 'That's not how it was at all.'

'Then how was it, Ruby, because I'm a little confused about what's going on here?'

He wasn't the only one. Her mind was such a jumble of emotions and feelings she felt dizzy. And worst of all she knew that she couldn't share any of that with him. 'Perhaps we could talk about it later,' she volunteered, wanting time to sort out some sort of strategy where Sam was concerned. 'After work.'

'Oh, yes, of course. Work. Your favourite crutch.' His lips twisted into a hard slant. 'Well, not this time, Ruby. We've played by your rules long enough. Now we play by mine.'

'My rules?' Ruby said incredulously. 'How can you say that? I've done everything you asked of me.' She'd set every weekend aside for him, not making any plans that didn't include him, or that couldn't be changed at the last minute. She'd kept her phone close and waited for him to call—longed for him to call. She'd dreamed of him, missed him, given her heart to him... 'I've given you everything you wanted.'

'Hardly, angel,' he dismissed scathingly. 'But none of that matters now. All that does is this.' He stabbed a finger at the transfer notice that lay on her desk between them. 'And whether you want me to sign off on it or not.'

Tell me you don't want to sign it, she pleaded silently. *Tell me you want me to stay here. With you.*

The unexpected thought caught her unawares, tightening her throat. Should she tell him what she was thinking? Should she open up and admit how she felt about him?

An ancient argument between her parents came rushing back to her. She'd been about to ask her father to help with her maths homework while her parents were sitting at the kitchen table. Then her father had stood up, shaking his head, accusing her mother of being too needy, too clingy. Ruby had witnessed her mother's devastation, her utter helplessness, as she'd begged her father not to leave her. He'd done so anyway and Ruby had made a silent vow that no man would ever be able to accuse her of the same thing. That she would never want a man more than he wanted her. And yet that was exactly how she felt right now. History repeating itself one generation on.

Swallowing hard, she shoved back the tears that threatened to clog her throat and lifted her chin. 'Why wouldn't I want you to sign off on it?' she asked crisply.

A muscle flicked in Sam's jaw. 'Well, that's the million-dollar question, isn't it, angel? And frankly I can't think of a single good reason why you wouldn't.'

CHAPTER TEN

'LET ME SEE if I've got this straight,' Dante drawled, sitting on the barstool beside him. 'You asked her if she wanted you to sign the transfer papers and then you signed them without waiting for her answer? How does that work exactly?'

'I didn't need to wait for her answer. Her silence was telling.' Sam looked between Dante and Tino and wondered which one of them was more stupid. 'She wouldn't have applied for it if she didn't want to go.'

'But you signed it and you don't want her to go.'

'I didn't say that.' Sam took another sip of his beer. He'd known it would be a mistake to come out with his brothers straight after his altercation with Ruby, but they hadn't exactly given him a choice. After he'd stormed out of Ruby's office he'd found both brothers at the bank of lifts, waiting for him. Having just flown down from Brisbane, Dante had met with Tino and they'd descended on Sam with the express purpose of taking him for a drink. He'd told them that he wasn't fit company for anyone right now and that had sealed his fate. Of course they had wanted to know why.

Now he was in the same pub that he'd met Ruby in two years ago, propping up the bar and forced to fill his brothers in on what had happened, and so far they weren't happy with the abridged version.

'Didn't have to say it,' Dante said, lobbing a peanut into his mouth. 'You wouldn't be upset at signing it if you'd wanted to.'

'Thanks for the analysis, Dr Freud. Can we move on now?' Sam could feel himself getting more and more riled by his thickheaded older brothers, and if they weren't careful he'd bite.

'Dante's right,' Tino put in. 'If you wanted to sign it, you'd be fine with it.'

'Do either of you idiots realise how close I am to taking this conversation outside? With the both of you?'

'Could be fun,' Dante said. 'Like old times.'

'We could mess up his pretty face,' Tino agreed.

'Look who's talking, Boy Racer,' Sam muttered, calling Tino by Miller's pet name for him.

'Trying to get personal, junior?' Tino laughed.

'Trying to get you to shut up,' Sam griped.

'Oh, man,' Tino said softly. 'You're in trouble, aren't you?'

'I have no idea what you're talking about,' Sam said testily.

'Neither do I,' Dante drawled.

'He's in love.'

'In love?' Dante looked aghast. 'Not possible.'

'He's also still here,' Sam grumbled. 'And I'm not in love.' Why give his brothers more ammunition than they already had? 'I'm annoyed that I'm losing a good lawyer. One of the best in the firm to a place...to a place that's about as exciting as having your nails done.'

'Most women enjoy having their nails done,' Dante pointed out.

'Shut up, D.' Sam growled darkly. 'You don't know what you're talking about. The fact is why would she want to go anywhere else when everything she needs is right here?'

'Hell.' Dante gave Tino a look. 'I think you're right.'

'Dammit, you two. I already feel enough of a fool without either of you rubbing my face in it.'

Tino and Dante stared at him without speaking and he knew that both of them had the patience to wait him out. Well, Dante did; Tino's patience depended on his mood.

Finally Sam sighed. 'Okay, I'm in love with her. There. Happy? Can we move on now?'

'Sure,' Dante said, offering him a sympathetic grimace. 'I'd want to move on too if it were me.'

Only Sam realised that he wasn't ready to move on after all. 'You know, the stupid thing is that before this happened I was going to call you,' he told Tino. 'Ask you for advice.'

'You were going to call Tino for advice?' Dante's

expression was almost comical. 'I know more about women than he ever will.'

'*Knowing* more women than I do doesn't mean that you know more *about* them,' Tino corrected. 'What did you want to know?'

'Doesn't matter now.' Sam raised his glass to his lips, only to find it empty. 'The moment's passed. For good.'

Dante signalled the bartender. 'Another round. Or two. I have a feeling we're going to need a lot more alcohol to get through this.'

'Of course it matters,' Tino said. 'You need a plan to win her back.'

'Or another beer.' Dante pushed a fresh glass in front of him. 'Here, have this one.'

'I didn't *win* her in the first place and it would be pointless to try again. I told you, it's finished. *Finito. Terminado.* How many languages do you need me to say it in?'

The truth was, Ruby didn't need him. Not the way he needed her, and he wasn't going to grovel. Nor was he going to talk about it endlessly. 'How's the hotel business, D? Bought any new skyscrapers lately?'

'Forget Dante,' Tino instructed. 'We're not finished with you yet.'

'Maybe we should talk about me,' Dante noted. 'Because I don't know what the hell has happened to the both of you. You meet a pretty face, she plays hard to get and next thing you're—'

'Careful, Dante,' Tino warned. 'Your time will come.'

'If it ever does, promise me you'll nail me inside a coffin and plant an oak tree over my body.'

'With pleasure,' Sam growled. 'And Ruby's not like that. She didn't play hard to get. Well, actually she did.' He gave a rough laugh. 'If you knew how hard I had to work to... The trouble is, she's so damned prickly and defensive and argumentative. She over-thinks everything and she's an absolute control freak.'

'She sounds like a real peach,' Dante drawled.

Sam shook his head. 'You have no idea. The woman is impossible.'

'Glad you worked it out.' Dante downed his beer. 'Women are trouble and we lone bachelors need to stick together.'

'Right,' Sam agreed, taking another pull of his beer and thinking that it tasted like dirt. Why couldn't anyone make a decent beer any more?

'You are so screwed, Samuel,' Tino noted.

Sam glared at his brother. 'Just because you're married doesn't mean it works out for everyone. I'll be fine.'

'I get it, bro—it's hard to talk about your feelings. I know. I nearly made the same mistake with Miller.'

'You're wrong, Tino. I'm fine with expressing my feelings. I was very expressive when I turned up in her office. I nearly...' He'd nearly dragged her across her wide desk and kissed her until she told him she wanted no one else but him. Told him that she'd never leave him. 'Anyway… It's not me who can't express myself, it's Ruby. She's as closed as a clam and as soon as you get close to her she throws up an unscaleable wall.'

'So what did she say when you told her how you felt? When you told her that you loved her, and wanted to be with her?'

Sam shook his head. 'What are you talking about? I didn't tell her…' He glanced from one brother to the other, realisation dawning slowly. 'Hell. I'm an idiot.'

'The thing is,' Tino began quietly, 'our father didn't leave us with a great legacy. All those times he shut us out he made it pretty hard for any of us to talk about our feelings, let alone embrace them.' A muscle in Tino's jaw worked overtime. 'I remember how hard you worked to get him to notice you, brandishing your athletics trophies and academic awards whenever he came through the door, and then—it was just after your tenth birthday, I think—you stopped. It was like you just gave up. Closed yourself off.'

'Ninth,' Sam corrected, his gut knotted as he remembered being left at the track on his birthday. 'I realised that giving up was easier.'

'We all gave up. In our own way. But it didn't make any of us happy.'

'I don't know—it felt pretty good to me,' Dante said.

'That's because you're thickheaded.'

'Thickheaded?' Dante spluttered indignantly. 'No one's thicker than Samuel here. And anyway, don't make this about me! I'm not the one foolish enough to fall in love.'

Sam shook his head. He wanted to bop his brothers on the nose but he knew they were only trying to help. It was the way it had always been between them, and Sam had often wondered what he'd have done without them growing up.

'Tell her how you feel,' Tino urged quietly. 'It will probably be the biggest risk you'll ever take, but it's worth it.'

'Whatever you're going to do, you might want to decide sooner rather than later,' Dante murmured under his breath. 'A gorgeous blonde just walked into the pub and if I'm not mistaken she has your name written all over her. More's the pity.'

Sam swivelled around to face the main entrance, where three women stood, their eyes adjusting to the dim lighting, and one of them was his Ruby, looking like a vision.

'Miller!' Ruby growled, her eyes alighting on Sam sitting at the bar beside his two brothers as soon as she entered the pub. 'Please tell me you didn't know Sam would be here.'

When she'd called Miller and broken down over the phone her best friend had immediately called Molly and they had agreed to meet at their favourite bar. On the car trip over they'd pretty much heard the whole story. How she and Sam had agreed to a weekend-only affair, how she'd stupidly fallen in love with him and how she planned to move to London. Because what else could she do? Working in the same office as Sam was absolutely untenable under the circumstances. At least, it was for her.

Now she felt a sense of déjà vu tightening her insides because this was the exact same bar she'd met Sam in two years ago.

'Don't hate me,' Miller began sheepishly. 'But I might have known.'

'I don't hate you. But I might kill you,' Ruby promised. 'I already told you that he signed the transfer papers and told me that work was my favourite crutch. What did you think was going to happen by bringing us together like this?'

'I don't know. Something?'

'He might have a point about the whole work-as-a-crutch thing,' Molly offered.

'Molly?' Ruby gave her sister a furious look. 'Whose side are you on?'

'We're on yours, sweetie,' Miller soothed. 'That's why we're here.'

'You could tell him how you feel,' Molly offered.

'Tell him how I feel?' Ruby looked at her sister, aghast. 'Not everything turns out like a Disney movie, Molly. You should know that.'

'I'm taking back what I said about you being scared of commitment,' Molly muttered. 'I'm inserting the word *petrified* instead.'

'I wouldn't say anything else if I were you.' She jabbed a finger at her sister in exasperation. 'Since you were no doubt in on this plan to sabotage me like this, I'm going to replace you with a cat. At least pets are loyal.'

Before Ruby could think about turning around and walking back outside, Sam rose from his bar stool and prowled towards her, the merry after-work crowd seeming to automatically part to make way for him.

Her heart very nearly stopped as he came to a halt in front of her, his tie askew and his hair rumpled as if he'd run his hand through it a thousand times.

'I didn't know you were here,' she said, not wanting him to think that she had anything to do with this unwanted set up.

'I have no doubt about that,' he murmured in his black-velvet voice. 'But now that you are I'd like to talk to you.'

Forget his sexy voice, Ruby told herself, *and instead concentrate on how you're going to get over him. Properly this time.*

'I don't think that's a good idea.'

'Ruby!' Molly exclaimed, elbowing her in the ribs.

'Will you give us a few minutes?' Sam asked, smiling at the two traitors beside her.

'Of course,' they readily agreed, rushing over to join Tino and Dante at the bar and leaving them alone together.

Sam frowned as he took in the boisterous crowd. 'Let's take this into the beer garden. It's most likely quieter than in here.'

Wanting to ask him what 'this' was, but not sure she could speak without getting emotional, Ruby reluctantly let him take her hand and lead her outside. Whatever he had to tell her, she vowed to listen and say nothing. Then she'd walk away and never see him again. It would be better that way. There was really no need for him to know how badly she felt about how things had ended between them.

'You look pale,' he said, stopping beside a large potted fern that softened the brickwork on the building. 'Do you need to sit down?'

No. What she needed was him. She just couldn't tell him that. 'I'm fine, just…just say what you want to say. I'm ready.'

Or not.

'Hell, Ruby, you don't make anything easy for a man, do you?'

She didn't know what he meant by that because she was trying to make this as painless as possible for both of them.

'Look, Sam, we complicated things by having an affair and now we have to uncomplicate it. I get it.'

'Affair?' he said with quiet menace. 'Is that what you call it?'

'I don't know. Affair…fling…'

'Don't you dare say hook-up,' he warned. 'I hate that term.'

'I wasn't going to but I think I understand why you want to talk to me, and you don't have to worry. I'm not going to harass you, or cry all over you, or tell anyone what happened. Well, other than Miller and Molly but they won't say anything to anyone. I promise.'

'I'm not worried about office gossip, Ruby.' Frustration etched his tone. 'That was always your issue.'

'Well, if you're worried I'll make a nuisance of myself and want more from you, I won't. I would never do that. I would never behave like that.'

'Why not?'

Ruby frowned. 'Why not? Because who would want someone like that? Someone clingy and needy?'

'Sweetheart, I feel clingy and needy every time you get within two feet of me.'

'What?' She blinked up at him as if she hadn't heard him right. 'How...? You can't be serious.'

'I am.' And as if to prove it he leant down and kissed her, taking her mouth with a savage hunger that incited her own.

Ruby's hands fisted in his shirt as she melted against him, the chemistry between them immediately hitting combustion levels, as it always did when they were this close. Sam groaned as he thoroughly explored her mouth, reluctantly drawing back and grimacing as he glanced at the small round tables filled with people pretending not to notice them.

'I don't know what it is about you and public places, but you're hell on my self-control,' he complained. 'You always have been.'

Ruby didn't know whether to be insulted or thrilled by the admission, the after-effects of that kiss still messing with her brain. 'It's only Wednesday night,' she said. 'Friday night is the one we usually muck up.'

'Actually I'd say Friday night is our best night so far. Along with a couple of Saturdays and Sundays thrown in for good measure.'

'Sam,' she implored huskily. She wasn't in the mood for him to tease her, or try to get her to relax. Her emotions were too fragile to cope. Too raw. 'Please hurry up and tell me what you want.'

'Well, that's easy,' he said simply. 'I want you.'

Ruby felt slightly dizzy at his words. She knew he meant in bed and her heart broke a little because she wanted that too but she also wanted the rest. She wanted the fairy tale Molly was always spouting on about. The one that didn't exist. 'I'm sorry but I can't go there again,' she said on a rush, unconsciously wrapping her arms around her stomach. 'Please don't ask me to.'

Sam took a step back, his eyes dark. 'Is that because of the way I responded to your transfer to London? Because if it is I know I didn't handle it well.'

'It's not that.' She swallowed hard. 'I don't blame you for being upset about the transfer. You're my boss and I should have told you earlier.'

'I didn't get upset because I'm your boss, Ruby. I was upset because, while I had been sitting in my office trying to work out how to tell you that I love you, I imagined you were sitting in yours picturing how you were going to escape to London.'

Sam's words sent a shockwave through Ruby, turning her eyes wide. 'What did you say?'

'I love you. But I don't blame you for doubting me,' he said softly. 'I feel like I've been dancing around my feelings for you ever since we met. But I do love you, Ruby. With all my heart.' He took her trembling hands in his. 'It took me a while to recognise how I felt because I learned at a young age that it was easier to turn away from these kinds of feelings than it was to face them.'

'Because of your father.'

'Yes, and every time I thought you were putting work ahead of me it was like facing his rejection all over again. It made me want to protect myself. But I don't care about any of that now. I've had time to think about what it would mean to let you go and I don't want to. Ever. If you want to go to London then I'll go with you.'

Not expecting him to do anything like that for her, Ruby stared up at him. 'You'd really do that for me?'

'Ruby, don't you know by now that I'd do anything for you?' His eyes were full of love and heat as he looked at her. 'I love you more than I thought it was possible to love anyone. That day at the beach house when I asked you to marry me—'

'You were trying to get a rise out of me.'

'I was.' A wry smile tugged at his lips. 'A little, but as soon as I said it part of me knew I was also serious. I want you, Ruby. I want to be the man who makes you smile first thing in the morning and last thing at night, I want to be the one who makes you happier than you ever have been before and I want you beside me. Day and night. I want to know that when I get home from work you'll be there, and I have to believe that you want that too or I'll go mad.'

Ruby bit her lip, hardly daring to trust that any of this was real. 'Oh, Sam, I do. I do want that too, but—'

'You're scared.' He gently smoothed her hair back from her face. 'I get that, angel. I get that you have little faith in men and that I'm partly responsible for that, but let me make it up to you. Let me spend my days proving to you that men do keep their promises. That I keep mine.'

'That wasn't just your fault, Sam. You were right when you said I use work as a crutch. Work has always been my safety net. It was my vehicle to independence and self-sufficiency and it could never surprise me by wanting to move on when I least expected it.'

'You don't need a safety net with me, Ruby, because I'll never want to move on from you.'

'Oh, Sam, I love you so much.' Unable to contain her joy a moment longer, Ruby threw her arms around his neck. 'I think I fell in love with you right here two years ago because I could never forget you no matter how hard I tried.'

Sam shuddered against her. 'And thank God for

that because I couldn't forget you either. Now, about London—'

'I don't really want to move to London,' she interrupted.

'You don't?'

'No. I put in for a transfer when you joined the firm because I didn't think I could see you in the office every day and not want you. I didn't think I could cope if you turned up one day with another woman on your arm.'

'Little fool,' he admonished softly, kissing her so tenderly Ruby's heart felt as if it might burst out of her chest. 'Once I saw you again there's been no one but you. I love you, Ruby. Only you. I even bought the beach house near Miller and Tino because you loved it. It's in your name. I wanted to give it to you tonight.'

'What? That's crazy.'

'That's how you make me feel most of the time. Crazy and happy and… Why are you crying?'

'Am I crying?' Ruby swiped her fingers across the tears she hadn't realised were rolling down her face. 'Oh, Sam, I'm so happy. I had no idea I could ever feel like this!'

'As long as you only feel like this with me. For ever.'

'I do. I will.'

'Hold that thought.' He gathered her closer and pulled a small box out of his pocket. 'I saw this in LA and I can tell by the look on your face that you want to say no, but I want to marry you, Ruby. I want to marry you and prove to you that relationships are worth banking on. I want to show you how good we are together, and I want everyone to know that you're mine.'

'You're wrong, Sam—I don't want to say no, I want to say yes so badly I know that I shouldn't.'

'You definitely should.' He flipped open the box to reveal an enormous diamond ring sparkling inside.

'Oh, my...'

Sam cupped the nape of her neck and tilted her head back, his eyes full of a possessive heat that made her giddy. 'Oh, my, yes? Or oh, my, no?'

'Oh, my, yes,' Ruby whispered on a laugh. 'Oh, my, a thousand times yes.'

'Thank God.' Sam kissed her soundly and slid the ring onto her finger to a rousing applause from everyone around them. 'Because we belong together. We always have.'

Embarrassed to realise that she'd been so lost in the moment nothing else had existed except Sam, Ruby buried her face against his neck.

'I think I'd better get you home before I ravish you against an outdoor wall again,' Sam murmured, tucking her in against his side.

'Promise?'

He turned her in the circle of his arms and looked down at her. 'Sweetheart, I hereby promise to ravish you and love you for the rest of your life, no matter where we are.'

Ruby grinned and wrapped her arms around his neck. 'Then I promise to love you and ravish you right back.'

'God, I hope so.'

Ruby laughed at the hungry desperation in his voice. 'Do you think we should go inside and tell the others what's going on?'

Sam glanced over her shoulder and Ruby turned to see their small party raising a toast to them through the pub window. 'I think they've probably already guessed, love, and if I know Miller she's already been on the phone booking us a wedding venue.'

'I don't mind,' Ruby said. 'Do you?'

'Not a bit. You're mine now.' He drew her up onto her toes, his mouth hovering over hers. 'And not just for weekends or clandestine meetings outside at posh parties.'

'Okay.'

'You're mine for ever.'

'Okay.' Ruby entwined her arms around his neck and pulled his mouth down to hers. 'Whatever you say, Sam.'

Sam groaned. 'It feels like I've waited a long time to hear you say that and you're not even naked.'

Ruby laughed, happiness bubbling over inside her. 'Then what are you waiting for?' she whispered.

'Privacy,' Sam growled, swinging her up into his arms and carrying her out of the pub.

Ruby clung to his shoulders. 'I can't wait,' she said happily, knowing that she wasn't just talking about the night ahead, but also the rest of their lives together.

* * * * *

If you enjoyed
The Billionaire's Virgin Temptation
you're sure to enjoy these other stories
by Michelle Conder!

Defying the Billionaire's Command
Russian's Ruthless Demand
The Italian's Virgin Acquisition
Bound to Her Desert Captor

Available now!

#3713 CLAIMED FOR THE SHEIKH'S SHOCK SON
Secret Heirs of Billionaires
by Carol Marinelli

For Khalid, nothing compares to the bombshell that Aubrey's had his secret child! Claiming his son is non-negotiable for this proud prince... But claiming Aubrey will prove a much more delicious challenge!

#3714 A CINDERELLA TO SECURE HIS HEIR
Cinderella Seductions
by Michelle Smart

To secure his heir, Alessio will use his incredible chemistry with his nephew's legal guardian, Beth, and command her to marry him! But will their intensely passionate marriage be enough for this innocent Cinderella?

#3715 THE ITALIAN'S TWIN CONSEQUENCES
One Night With Consequences
by Caitlin Crews

Sarina's used to working with powerful men. But she isn't prepared for the fire billionaire Matteo ignites in her! Succumbing to indescribable pleasure changes everything between them. Especially when she discovers she's pregnant—with the Italian's twins!

#3716 PREGNANT BY THE COMMANDING GREEK
by Natalie Anderson

Leon can't resist indulging in a night of pleasure with Ettie! But her pregnancy bombshell demands action. Leon's heir will not be born out of wedlock, so Ettie must say "I do"...

#3717 PENNILESS VIRGIN TO SICILIAN'S BRIDE
Conveniently Wed!
by Melanie Milburne
Gabriel offers a simple exchange—for her hand in marriage he'll save Francesca's ancestral home. And their attraction can only sweeten the deal. But her secret innocence is enough to make Gabriel crave his wife—forever!

#3718 WEDDING NIGHT REUNION IN GREECE
Passion in Paradise
by Annie West
When Emma overhears Christo admitting he married her for convenience, she flees, not expecting him to follow—with seduction in mind! Will a night in her husband's bed show Emma there's more than convenience to their marriage?

#3719 MARRIAGE BARGAIN WITH HIS INNOCENT
by Cathy Williams
Matias never does anything by halves. So when Georgie confesses his family believes they're engaged, he'll ensure everyone believes their charade. But discovering Georgie's true innocence suddenly makes their fake relationship feel unexpectedly—deliciously!—real...

#3720 BILLIONAIRE'S MEDITERRANEAN PROPOSAL
by Julia James
To convince everyone he's off-limits, Tara will pose as billionaire Marc's girlfriend. But when the world believes they're engaged, becoming his fiancée pushes their desire to new heights! Dare Tara believe their Mediterranean fantasy could be real?

YOU CAN FIND MORE INFORMATION ON UPCOMING HARLEQUIN® TITLES, FREE EXCERPTS AND MORE AT WWW.HARLEQUIN.COM.

HPCNM0419RB

Get 4 FREE REWARDS!

We'll send you 2 FREE Books plus 2 FREE Mystery Gifts.

Harlequin Presents® books feature a sensational and sophisticated world of international romance where sinfully tempting heroes ignite passion.

FREE Value Over $20